Epoch-1

New and Collected Sci-Fi Stories

Desmond Astaire

King & Vagabond Press, LLC

The following titles were first published as follows:

"Cherenkov Time." In *ZNB Presents: Year One*, edited by Joshua Palmatier. Binghamton, NY: Zombies Need Brains, 2023.

"Gallows." In *Writers of the Future Volume 38*, edited by David Farland. Los Angeles: Galaxy Press, 2022.

"It's a Nash Equilibrium, Then." In *Fission 3*, edited by Eugen Bacon and Gene Rowe. Stoke-on-Trent, GB-ENG: The British Science Fiction Association, 2023.

"Obsidian Grackle." In *Murderbirds*, edited by Mike Jack Stoumbos. Midlothian, VA: WonderBird Press, 2023.

"Old Dean." In *HyphenPunk Magazine #9*. Johnson City, TN: HyphenPunk, 2023.

Paranorm. Morton, IL: King & Vagabond Press, 2023.

"The Otherworld Theory." In *Aurealis*, Vol. 162. Mount Waverley, Vic: Chimaera Publications, 2023.

"You Are the Mother of Doomsday." In *Murderbugs*, edited by Mike Jack Stoumbos. Midlothian, VA: WonderBird Press, 2024.

Reviews

What the Readers are Saying

"Pacy paranormal mystery laser-targeted for those of us who grew up on *Buffy*, *Angel*, and *The X-Files*."
–J.L. George, author of *The Word* and New Welsh Writing Award recipient

"Desmond Astaire creates another intriguing read that is fast paced with a satisfying ending."
–N.V. Haskell, author of "Out There With Them," *Robotic Ambitions* and Writers of the Future winner

"Heart-pounding science fiction that will keep you in its grip from beginning to end. A true joy to read."
–Ryan Cole, Writers of the Future winner

"A rising talent in science fiction and fantasy with a promise of much more to come!"
–Shannon Fox, author of *Empire's Song* and recipient of Colorado Book Award for Best Anthology

"For lovers of *The Twilight Zone*." –Tangent Online

"If Hitchcock had done sci-fi, he would have done something like this."
–Goodreads review

You never know how you will impact the flow of time.

My upmost gratitude to—

Dean Wesley Smith, whose work inspired a child to start writing short stories;

Dr. Chris Johnson, for reading everything I've ever written since the beginning;

Lindsey, my beloved partner in turning the world's dreams to reality;

the generous Galaxy Press and Writers of the Future, who first published me;

Kevin J. Anderson, Dr. Doug Beason, Dr. Gregory Benford, Orson Scott Card, David Farland, Eric Flint, Brian Herbert, Nina Kiriki Hoffman, Nancy Kress, Katherine Kurtz, Todd McCaffrey, Rebecca Moesta, Larry Niven, Jody Lynn Nye, Dr. Nnedi Okorafor, Tim Powers, Kristine Kathryn Rusch, Brandon Sanderson, Dr. Robert J. Sawyer, Robert Silverberg, Dean Wesley Smith, S.M. Stirling, and Dr. Sean Williams,
whose expertise played a role in setting everything in motion.

Contents

PREFACE

This book represents the culmination of the first generation of my storytelling adventures. They were written over a period of four years, and rereading each one slings me back to a different emotion and memory in time. May your anchors in time always glow with warmth.

I still cherish each of these stories like a father admiring his growing family. I gave birth to them. I raised them the best I knew how to. And then I sent each one of them out into the world, with both pride and fear. I hope they touch something in people's souls. These stories are part of me, and now you.

Master music producer Rick Rubin said it best: "I'm not making it for [the audience]. I'm making it for me. And, it turns out, that when you make something truly for yourself, you're doing the best thing you possibly can for the audience." I thoroughly enjoyed these stories, and I hope you do as well.

Thank you for sharing the world with me, and I hope to see you next time, too.

With thanks,

-Des

What am I now that I was then?
May memory restore again and again
The smallest color of the smallest day:
Time is the school in which we learn,
Time is the fire in which we burn.

Delmore Schwartz

CHERENKOV TIME

It should take somewhere around 7.2 exajoules of energy to stop time, according to my internet math. That's the power of thirty-four Russian nukes going off at the same time, but somehow nature built my body to harness it. I can't explain that, don't try to, and I sure as hell am not going to let a government lab try and figure it out. There's only one person (and you) who knows that I can stop time and I'd like to keep it that way. I don't do it often because the aftermath makes an *I'll-never-drink-again* hangover seem like the sniffles.

There were a good handful of short stops here and there that didn't wreck me. I got pretty good at those. But the big ones, I wrote those down in the journal. I tried to get the times right for you.

The first time was December 3rd, 2013, south side of Chicago, when that guy almost put a bullet in me during an arrest. *Almost.* A few more minutes in the void and Time would've killed me and I never would've known it.

There were more times than I want to count later that month at Glace Bay University Medical Center. Medical tests over and over and over, trying to figure out what was making me sick. I thought I was going to die right there on the exam table. Turns out we found out how to keep me alive.

August 19th, 2019, River North Hospital, when I met my newborn son and the terror of caring for another life finally landed. I told myself I'd take just a few minutes to process it. That fear turned into unconditional love so quickly.

And now. September 12th, 2021, Lake Geneva, Wisconsin. The police department puts on family retreat weekends, usually at a waterpark lodge type of place. We do bonding activities and resiliency workshops during the day with the chaplains, then dine and swim with our fellow cop families in the evenings.

My cell phone rings while I help Chaplain Dan set up the conference room for the day's workshops.

"Tucker, I, uh, I c-can't find Will."

It's Riya, but I've never heard that shaking in her voice before.

"What do you mean, 'You can't find Will?'" I ask.

"I was taking a shower a-a-and he was watching cartoons on the couch and the door was open w-when I got out."

"How long ago?"

"Twenty minutes, I think."

Shit.

"Okay, baby, stay calm. Where have you looked so far?"

"I swear, I didn't think he could reach the door handle. I—" Her voice cracks and she collapses into loud, desperate sobs. "*Tucker, I can't find Will!*"

Chaplain Dan overhears the commotion. He's concerned. I don't have time to explain.

"Riya, where have you looked?" I'm trying to stay calm, but the adrenaline is kicking in. There's a snap in my voice.

"Uh, umm, the room, the entire room, the h-hallway, the top of the stairwell. There's a family up here. They didn't see him. Oh god, please, oh god."

I'm not so worried about how far a two-year-old can get, more about what happens to him when he's there.

The conference room is near the lobby. I can see outside. Unfamiliar faces checking out, loading their cars. Cars leaving the resort and turning onto the highway. Thick woods and ravines surrounding the property. Today's supposed to be a low of forty degrees and it's raining.

I pull out my special watch, wrap it around my wrist, and ready my thumb on the starter button. I've got one jump-start syringe in my pocket—just one. The next delivery won't arrive until Tuesday.

"Stay right there, Riya. I'm coming up."

I clench my fists, flexing whatever mystery muscle is up there in my head until I start to see the blue glow surround me, then everything goes silent. Sound doesn't travel in the void of timelessness.

December 3rd, 2013

It doesn't take long for a rookie cop to get indoctrinated into the rotted streets of the Windy City. I'd been working midnights on a South Side beat for two years and had already seen enough to jade me. Not many surprises anymore. I don't know why that night in particular was different.

"232-Robert."

"232-Robert, go Squad."

"Received a report of an armed robbery at Washington Park Pharmacy. Suspect is one white male, black coat, blue watch cap over braids, tattoos on face and neck. Victim reported the suspect showed a revolver, took a prescription bottle, and fled on foot southbound on Michigan Avenue."

"10-99, Squad. On my way from South Indiana and East 57th."

"10-4."

"232, 225. Let me know your 20. I'll meet you there."

"Copy."

Nine times out of ten I'd show up on-scene, take a good report, we'd put out a "Be on the Lookout" message to the other patrol units, and (statistically speaking) that'd probably be the end of it. But not that night.

Sure enough, the suspect turned the corner of the Michigan Avenue liquor store right as I came up to the intersection. He was a tall, lanky kid, not much younger than me. Unmistakable. I wasn't running my lights or sirens, so I saw him before he saw me. I called it in, flipped on the berries and cherries, and gunned the accelerator. Whipping my cruiser into the store's back lot gave the suspect two options: backtrack into the open intersection where I or my backup could more easily take him down on foot or try to go through me and disappear into the residential area behind us.

There's always that fraction of a second where you can see a suspect freeze and their instinct decides what's going to happen next. My guy decided on Option Two, but I was an all-state running back in high school.

He made it across the lot and into the alley before we collided against an iron fence for the fight. I made a mistake. I should've pulled my stun gun while we were sprinting. I suppose it wouldn't have mattered anyway because when I did get a chance to break away from him and fire it off, nothing happened. I saw the laser light on his chest and heard the unmistakable electric crackle, but the suspect ripped the darts right off his jacket as soon as they landed.

It was the jacket: it was too thick. The darts didn't pierce through. And it was at that moment that the suspect took out *his* weapon. I felt a tingle of panic charge up my temples the instant I saw the glimmer of the steel revolver peek out from his pocket.

"Drop your weapon!" Raw instinct. My left palm went up, my right hand down to my pistol. My regular holster broke the week earlier, so I was using my backup—a model referred to as a "suicide holster" due to a propensity for its flap hook to get stuck. Which is exactly what happened.

The suspect had his gun all the way out and I was still fumbling for mine. It was all over now. I knew it.

"No. *No. Stop!*"

The suspect leveled his gun on me and I felt something in my chest. Not pain or terror, but heat. An energy. Something solid. I was sure he had pulled the trigger and I was about to die, because I could see a heavenly light enveloping me.

The suspect froze, his gun still trained right on me, but I was somehow still standing. So I ripped my holster open, pulled my firearm, and squeezed the trigger. Nothing happened.

Nothing happened.

But of course, I didn't realize this at first due to the adrenaline surging through my blood. My first clue should have been the suspect's stuck, twisted expression. What was he waiting for? Maybe he was stoned out of his mind. Maybe he was having second thoughts. I didn't waste any time figuring it out.

I yanked the revolver out of his hand, secured it in my belt, and pulled his arms behind his back to handcuff them. He was stiff as starch.

"On your knees, *now.*"

He didn't comply, so I applied pressure to the back of his knee and leaned him backward. He stayed rigid.

"Come on, man, get on..."

It was then I realized it wasn't *him* that wasn't complying. It was gravity. It had just *stopped*. So had sound. So had movement. Everything. My patrol car's lights—usually rotating red and blue—were stuck on blue. It made it difficult to see the blue, aura-like glow following me everywhere I went. But it made it easy to see the bullet hovering right where I had been standing.

I knelt in front of it to get a better look. There was no blood on it, no disfigurement, so it hadn't hit me. All of which was great, but didn't even begin to answer why it was suspended mid-air. In the middle of all of it, my eyes trained on some dark, disembodied shadow person strobing its away across the lot toward me, blipping in and out of existence. Freakiest nightmare fuel I'd ever seen.

I knew it couldn't be real. This had to be a seizure or purgatory, maybe a catatonic dream or coma—something I could let go of and wake up from.

Something about that realization worked because that bullet I was eyeballing came back to life right then. It ripped across my cheek and knocked me down, but the agonizing heartbeat pounding out of my chest, violent tremors, and complete muscle failure kept me from getting back up.

And then the suspect was standing over me, kicking my already nauseated stomach over and over again.

"How'd you do that? *How'd you do that, man?*"

He looped his cuffed hands around his legs, yanked me to my feet, pinned me against the fence, and put my own gun to my forehead. It was searing hot against the sweat I was raining, but I was too crippled to fight back.

"What just happened?" he pleaded through grit teeth. I was slipping in and out of consciousness, fighting a crushing fatigue, but I distinctly remember his eyes were glossy. It was terror. "How did you do that?" he begged.

POP, POP, POP, POP!

I collapsed to the ground along with the suspect.

"225-Robert, 11-41, officer down, East 56th and Michigan!"

It was my partner, Darnell.

"Tuck, where are you hit?" He ripped my shirt open and patted down my bulletproof vest for entry wounds. "Tuck, talk to me, bro. Jesus, you're burning up."

"Not...shot. Thirsty...thirsty." It hurt to make words through cotton mouth and sandpaper lips, but stronger than that was my body desperately screaming for hydration.

Darnell rubbed some snow across my forehead, put a little bit in my mouth, and it helped me stay conscious for a few moments.

"Stay awake, Tuck. You're gonna be okay. You're gonna be okay." I think Darnell was saying it more for himself than for me.

That was the first time I stopped the clock. After that, I'd get better at controlling the side effects, but that crash would never let me forget the inevitable cost of such a power.

Present

I sprint down the hotel hallway and up the back stairs, instinctively making mental notes of everything I see—a perk of the job. The blue shadow glow following me is a byproduct of moving through stopped time and it will help mark where I've already searched for my boy. Thankfully, we're staying on the second floor. Even more fortunately, the elevator doors are open for a family getting ready to go down to the pool.

There's no sign of Will. None.

Our hotel room door is propped open by the swing bar lock, which is great because my electronic keycard wouldn't work in the void. Riya is on the couch with her head in her hands. She's a good mother. She's just scared. I want to stop and whisper to her that everything will be okay, but I can't afford that luxury. Time is actually a commodity in timelessness.

I look at my stopwatch and it reads ninety-six seconds timeless. That's two days and some change aged.

I tear into all the places a toddler could hide in an extended stay hotel suite—inside cabinets, under furniture, behind curtains. Not a lot of real estate. My heart kicks at each new hiding spot in hopes of finding that giant smile holding up squishy cheeks and bright eyes.

Nothing.

The hotel room is a bust, along with the elevator and a stairwell. There's no time to sacrifice to second-guessing. I have to keep moving. There's a second stairwell at the far end of the hallway and that's my next target. My head pulsates and buzzes as I begin losing the battle of paternal panic. I can't think straight, can't recall what my police training would tell me to do next. But my worst fears say to start looking in the cars leaving the resort.

I reach to my belt behind my right hip to double-check that I'm carrying my duty pistol. It's there, right next to the last jump-start injection, and I'm definitely going to need it now.

The stopwatch says it's been three minutes, nine seconds timeless. Six days aged.

December 16th, 2013

All the hospital doctors could diagnose was that I wasn't going to die. So, they cut me loose and sent me to a week's worth of Chicagoland medical specialists who also couldn't give me any answers worth a damn.

I *didn't* have porphyria, autoimmune disease, diabetic ketoacidosis, hypothermia, sepsis, or drug abuse. My symptoms did, however, fit the bill of a "thyroid storm," but still meant squat because I had no other indicators of a hyperactive thyroid. All the docs' answers were the same. "All we can do is wait and see if it happens again." All except for one at the Glace Bay University Medical Center neuroendocrinology department, a medical resident on exchange from Oxford.

Dr. Shah looked like she wanted to jump out of her skin at her attending physician's non-answer but was strategic enough not to. She did, however, conspicuously walk me down the hall out of earshot of her superiors in order to make an actual elevator pitch.

"Officer Sims, I believe there may be an answer—an unconventional answer—to your symptoms," she said.

"Okay. What is it?"

"I could get in a lot of trouble for...but, well, you see, my interests are in quantum biology—the subatomic components of the body's energy conversion processes. I analyzed your blood sample over the weekend and discovered there is a very recent trauma to the DNA methylation of your CpG dinucleotides—a type of trauma I've never, ever seen before."

"I'm a cop, doc. You're going to need to break that down Barney-style for me."

"Your body's epigenetic clock is...wrong," she said. "At a cellular level, you're slightly older than you should be, but there's no medical reason *why*. I don't even know how I could recreate the anomaly if I tried. Did *something* happen to you that you haven't told the other doctors?"

The elevator lights counted down the floors one by one, a "ding" piercing the silence with each passing floor.

"I thought I was hallucinating," I said. "You're going to think I'm crazy."

"There's a lot of latitude for imagination in my field of study," Doc Shah said. "I'm going crazy myself trying to figure this out on my own."

I took Doc Shah to the alley down by South Michigan and East 56th and walked her through the whole story from beginning to end. It ended with her eyes wide and staring. It was twenty degrees outside, snowing, and we were now a few steps outside "latitude for imagination."

"You *stopped* time?" she asked. "You must understand, I need some kind of proof of this hypothesis."

"Okay. How?"

"Cherenkov radiation."

"What's that?"

"The blue glow," Doc Shah said. "If everything you say is true, then the blue glow was Cherenkov radiation generated by your body moving faster than the phase velocity of light in stopped time. Prove it by making the glow again. Draw something in the sky with your finger."

"What if I get sick again?"

"Then I'll call an ambulance."

"I'm not even sure how I did it," I said.

"Then, Officer Sims, without—"

"Tucker. Please."

"Then, Tucker, without a replication, I can't help you, even if I believed you. I'm sorry."

I could feel that tinge of panic erupt in my chest and creep up behind my neck. Right then, Doc Shah was the closest thing I had to an answer, and she was seconds from walking away. So I grabbed onto that feeling and clung to it for leverage.

"What do you want me to draw?" I asked.

Doc Shah placed her hands behind her back.

"How many fingers am I holding up?" she asked.

I clenched my fists—not quite sure what that was supposed to do—and recalled how I felt at the moment of the shooting.

"*Right now.* This very second," she demanded.

I felt a warmth erupt in my chest. It was happening again. I gritted my teeth and willed the sensation to the surface.

"*What's the number, Officer Sims?*"

The energy radiated from my core, out my limbs, and then everything was quiet. Pure, absolute silence. I opened my eyes to frozen time—every speck of snow, every plume of car exhaust, Doc Shah mid-yell—all suspended in a moment.

I ran over to check behind her back and rushed back to my starting point to draw the number "4" in the air, just about running through an out-of-place shadow I hadn't noticed before. I dodged it, tripped over myself, and fell to the ground in a defensive stance. It was the same dark figure I'd seen when I got shot.

It strobed less and moved a bit faster this time. It was more refined now, too—closer to the shape of a body with an arm stretched out to grab me, but still transparent and flickering like a neon light gone bad. But it was three-dimensional. This thing was a *something*.

Ghost, Angel of Death, *bhūta*, whatever—I didn't want to mess around and find out. I rose to a knee and braced myself for the beating I was about to take on reentry. Unlike last time, I was now aware of a tension—like a flexed muscle—through my whole body. I let go of the tension and, sure enough, everything around me returned to life.

Rather than the body slam of life being sucked out of me, I was just hit with fatigue, like before your head hits the pillow. It only took a few moments to shake it off and stand to my feet, quite amused at the pleasant surprise. Doc Shah was experiencing her own bout of shock, slack-jawed confusion, and wonder.

"Oh my," she muttered. "Brilliant. Just brilliant."

Her eyes were locked on the contour of the number four hidden within the flowing midst of fading, cerulean blue swirls.

"Hey, Doc?" I asked after a minute.

Doc Shah's eyes floated over to me. "You're not sick?"

"I feel like I just worked an entire shift in thirty seconds. But no, this isn't like the first time. No need to call in the cavalry."

"Good...good." She nodded, her mind preoccupied. "I need to get you to my lab. And call me Riya."

December 31st, 2013

Riya answered her apartment door with a bottle of champagne in hand.

"Little early to start the festivities, isn't it?" I asked.

"This is for a different celebration," she said.

"Oh, yeah?"

Riya pulled me into her hobby lab in the spare room and started waving around her dry-erase board. It was marked up with wild line graphs and data points. To her, it was scientific gold, but I remembered the experiments as running a marathon of gauntlets in and out of timelessness with varying physical side effects.

"I found the correlation," Riya said. I couldn't see it. "It's exponential. The longer you stay in stopped time, the more severely you age on the cellular level. That's why the damage to your telomeres varies every time. Twenty seconds timeless may just feel like twelve hours aged, but five minutes would equate to more than twenty-two days. Without water, nutrition, or sleep for that amount of equivalent time, you could die as soon as you reentered normal time. *That's* why you experienced the physiological crisis on December 3rd."

"So, what, just stay under five minutes, or I'll die?" I asked.

"That's where this comes in," Riya said, pulling out a sealed glass vial of fluid. "I've developed a compound of potassium, magnesium, and adrenaline suspended in rapid-expanding normal saline."

You'd think from the amount of time we'd been spending together that she'd learn to speak plain English to me by now, but I just couldn't be frustrated at how excited she got. I just grinned to let her know there was no light bulb going off.

"Jump-start juice," she said. "One injection of this immediately after reentering time and all the side effects will be neutralized within minutes. It may be a rocky few minutes, but you'll live."

I walked up to the whiteboard, where the fourteen-minute data point was circled vigorously in red.

"What happens after fourteen minutes?"

She was not, however, excited about that data point, and her voice dropped low. "If you stay in timelessness for more than fourteen-and-a-half consecutive minutes, you'd age at least forty years and likely face instant biological death upon reentry."

I turned around to see her holding out a small gift-wrapped box.

"However, *this* will help prevent that," she said with a big smile. "Merry Christmas, Tucker."

I gave her the "you really shouldn't have" look, but she insisted. Inside the box was something I'd carry with me for the rest of my life: a simple, brass pocket watch with two analog faces on it, housed in an elastic wristband. One face said "Timeless" and counted from zero to fifteen in minutes. The inset face read "Aged" in days, then months, then years.

"The internal components are triggered electronically by the body's bioenergy field," Riya said. "As long as those two prongs on the bottom touch your skin, it should work even in timelessness. That way, you'll never get lost."

Riya never revealed my secret, not for all the world's promises of grants, fellowships, or awards. She always called me "Patient Kāla" (Sanskrit for "time") in her research papers. She never did figure out how, exactly, I was able to stop time. Something about an ability to manipulate the position of an elementary particle that hadn't been discovered yet. But she did teach me how to live with it.

Present

I make it down the second stairwell and sprint down a hallway back to the lobby, darting around bodies suspended in motion. Everything looks normal, as it should. Families are heading to the resort restaurant for breakfast or the indoor water park to start the day's festivities. No one has a care in the world except me.

I hit the brakes before reaching the main entrance and dash through the resort office on the desperate chance my son is there. I picture him sitting in the manager's office, bouncing and smiling in an oversized chair under the care of the resort staff without a care in the world, just waiting for his mommy and daddy to come discover him. The only thing in the office is disappointment and the absence of staff members. No time to second guess. Got to keep moving.

About three dozen cars are parked in the main entrance's immediate vicinity. My stopwatch reads five minutes, four seconds timeless. Twenty-three days aged. No time to search them all, so I do a quick scan for anyone that looks remotely familiar. I know that after family perpetrators, the second most common type of kidnapping is by acquaintances.

I see nothing. Nothing.

There are two vehicles leaving the parking lot, a minivan and a hatchback. I use a minute to run to them and do a quick assessment of the interior like I've done so many times during traffic stops. There's no sign of my son. But there is one sedan at the end of the resort's drive, about to turn onto the road to Highway 50. I estimate it's about 300 feet away—a price to pay no matter how fast I run. But what if Will is in that car? I don't need to think twice.

I summon the spirit of my high school sportsman's stamina, make the mad dash to the vehicle, and reach it in seventeen seconds, according to my stopwatch. I collapse against the car. My heart feels like it's trying to exit my chest, but I pull myself together enough to search the back seats, then the front. It's a little old lady driving. Not exactly the typical demographic profile of a kidnapper. But I'm not leaving until I see the inside of that trunk.

I have no tools I can use to pry it open, and I already know the electronic trunk release won't work in timelessness either. I try to open the rear doors to pull down the passenger seats, but the car is in drive, so the doors are locked. I resolve that with a window punch on the bottom of the multitool I always carry. The quarter glass window splinters away after a few strikes, and I've committed vehicle vandalism. I don't have time to weigh the morality of the decision, and I carefully navigate the shards away to unlock the rear door manually.

I pull down the passenger seat to reveal the trunk and see nothing but a few pieces of luggage and jumper cables—a complete bust. The little old lady will never know what happened. When time resumes, I'll be long gone, and her insurance will cover it as a rock or bird strike. My clock is ticking. Six minutes, forty-three seconds timeless. Fifty-one days aged.

I've got about five minutes before the aging becomes too exponential not to notice. Three hundred feet back, then what? I look back to the hotel and it feels like I'm stranded in an ocean looking back at the shore that's gotten too far away from me.

Where is my child?

Ocean. Water. Pool.

I didn't check the pool yet. *Christ, the swimming pool.*

August 19th, 2019

The neonatal doctor held you up with one hand, pointed with the other, and rattled off everything about a newborn like he was showing off the features of a new car. I didn't hear a word he said. All my attention diverted to this little being, only minutes new into this world, who looked as confused and bewildered as I felt. Riya was out of commission getting patched up after an emergency C-section, so it was just you and me. I was responsible for you and I had no clue what I was doing. Before I knew what was happening, the doctor stopped rambling and passed you over to me. I froze time.

I didn't know how to hold a baby. I didn't know what the difference between a diaper cry and a hungry cry was. I didn't know how to raise a child into an adult.

But there you were—just you and me. As soon as I restarted time, you were going to open your eyes and I'd be the first person you'd see. You needed me. And I was hiding in the void of timelessness like a coward. That same strobing shadow I always see in timelessness made its appearance in the hallway, without form and moving in slow motion. I still didn't know what it was, but it was terrifying, and it reminded me that you can't ever actually stop Time. You can only work with it the best you can.

I counted down: five, four, three, two, one…

And your raspy, rattling cries pierced the emergency room.

"It's okay, Will," I told you. I pulled you close into my arms and found the rhythm of the rock you liked best. "I love you, son. Daddy's here. Daddy's here. I've got you."

And I swear, you heard my voice and stopped crying for just a bit.

Present

I think there's a moment in the onset of true hopelessness where your blood actually stops flowing. My head is light, but my feet are heavy, and the sprint back to the lodge feels like a disassociated nightmare.

Most people don't know that CPR only has a fifteen percent success rate. But in this timeless moment, when I enter the lodge's swimming pool area, my boy is neither dead nor alive. He just *is*.

His eyes are closed and his lips are blue. There is no expression on his face as a staff member applies compressions to Will's sternum. My knees buckle under me and I collapse next to him, choking on tears and arrested breath.

There are lots of people at the pool. Parents. Kids. They probably all assumed Will was there with another family. The same people probably presumed he was playing with the other kids when he jumped into the pool. No one knew my child was alone until he didn't come up from under the water. But now I'm here.

I can't make time go backward, but I can keep it from going forward again.

I look at my stopwatch one last time. It reads eleven minutes and whatever seconds timeless. Four years aged. The years will come exponentially now with each passing minute—eight, sixteen, thirty-two, sixty-four, one-hundred-twenty-eight. I wonder what will happen when my body reaches the age of biological death. Will time resume with a poof of my dusted remains? Will time stay frozen forever?

You don't give me a chance to find out.

"Dad?"

I barely register your voice as ultimate grief rips my heart apart. I suppose your voice is just my brain shutting down upon the corona of death. But then I feel your hand on my shoulder. A dark, shadowy aura surrounds it—strobing, flickering in and out of time—but I can actually see you this time.

"You have no idea how hard it was to find you," you say. Your voice is echoey. Right next to me, but distant.

I realize you're real and spin up to my feet. You're translucent, here but not, yet I can still tell you're tall, strong, maybe a little older than me. You grab ahold of me, keeping me from backing into the pool.

"Dad, you're not hallucinating, but you *are* dying. Look me in my eyes and listen to me closely," you say, pointed and direct. I can tell you've rehearsed this many times. There's something about your voice that I intrinsically trust. You sound like me. You still have your mom's amber eyes. Presuming you're not just an illusion of my oxygen-starved, dying brain.

"I'm Will. I survive this. But I grow up without a father because you never leave the void. The people here say they saw a bright, blue aura of light surrounding me. They say it was a guardian angel, but I know it was you—the Cherenkov radiation."

"How is this possible?" I cry. "You grew up? You're like me?"

"Mom helped me figure this all out, but what I really needed was *my dad*. It's genetic, but there's so much more to it. I've been trying to find you in the voids, but this is the only timestamp that's worked."

The shadow figures. They were you all along?

How the hell does one jump into a stopped moment in time? But maybe you were just a few nanoseconds off target every time, and maybe that's why I couldn't see you clearly. I can't even begin to comprehend what it could've taken for you to land that perfect fraction of a second successfully. But I hold your face in my hand, and you're here now. I don't care if this is real or a delusion. I am so proud of you.

"Dad, *this is our last chance*," you say. "Please, Dad, go back. Every second counts."

I look at my stopwatch. You're right. I'll be in my late 40s now.

"I need you, Dad. *Please* go back."

I pull the jump-start syringe out of my pocket and ready it at my hip, still terrified that this is a figment of my body's imagination, a result of the life force being expended from my body, and that my baby boy will be passed on when I arrive.

But the desperation on your grown-up face is real. I love you, son. I'm here. I've got you.

I let go.

"Cherenkov Time" was first published in Joshua Palmatier's ZNB Presents *magazine (Zombies Need Brains; February 1, 2023) and the* ZNB Presents: Year One *anthology (Zombies Need Brains; July 1, 2023). The story was inspired by one of those traumatic events parents sometimes experience: We learned our toddler could reach door handles when he vanished from our hotel room while my wife was in the shower and I was downstairs helping set up a workshop. He was found safe soon after, trying to make his way down the stairwell on his own adventure. But the terror o f what-if planted itself in my head and percolated until a story formulated that made me consider: What would I have done—what would I have sacrificed—in that moment to find my son? Everything.*

Don't Speak to the Children

Clifford Caplan blew past the speed limit signs without regard to disturbing his suburbia. He was in real trouble this time. It was one thing to be late from work. He'd done that enough to have grown callous to his wife's resentment. It was another thing altogether to be late on Halloween. The sun was minutes—seconds—from dipping below the horizon. His cellphone sounded the alert for 5:44 p.m. Ninety seconds to nightfall on October 31st in the Midwest.

Stupid, stupid, stupid!

Clifford stomped the accelerator down and let the engine scream. His house was a mere two blocks away, and he hadn't yet seen any children on the streets. There was still time. He pumped the brakes at his house and fishtailed the car into the driveway. The sedan screeched to a jarring stop in front of the front door, which was already open. Clifford lunged through it, slammed it shut, and punched in the security code. All the doors and windows deadbolted shut as Clifford lost his footing and slipped onto his rear end in a final display of humiliation.

Sara stood in the kitchen—arms crossed, hip planted, jaw locked. Her eyes were always stone, but her current state of pissed-offness was especially frigid. Clifford had no excuse, but at least he was smart enough to admit it this time. There was *no* good reason for being late on Halloween.

The vacuum of silence trickled away to children's chirping outside, and dread replaced Sara's fury. Mascara-soaked tears seeped from her eyes when she couldn't keep her lip from shaking anymore, giving way to a burst of ugly sobs. She threw the tumbler of pink Himalayan salt at Clifford, and he finished the perimeter line in front of the doorway before offering his wife a long, apologetic embrace. He knew he'd hit the high score of jackassery tonight.

"I'm sorry. I'm sorry, babe," Clifford said. "It was irresponsible of me to cut it so close."

"I thought you were dead. I thought you were *gone*," Sara cried. "I couldn't close the door until you were home. I couldn't do it."

"I know. I'm here now," Clifford said. "We're completely safe. No evil spirits are going to take us this Halloween."

Smoldering white sage and extra large glasses of red wine mellowed the edge as Clifford and Sara simmered in their living room. Nightfall commenced without delay, but they'd always found it near impossible to sleep knowing everything outside was plotting to steal your soul. So, the couple binge-streamed some show for mindless background noise; the only thing broadcast television would be playing for the next thirteen-and-a-half hours was a shelter-in-place order.

An aggressive knock on the door shattered the calm, and Clifford and Sara jumped up as if the couch had short-circuited. They knew it had to be coming sooner or later, but there wasn't a way to psychologically prepare.

"Trick or treat!" a chorus of little voices called from the other side of the door. They could make out the monstrous, discorded undertones hidden under cherub voices in their breathless silence.

"Shit!" Sara said. The refrigerator was next to the front door, and the bowl of assorted candy was on top. "I didn't put the bowl out. *Shit!*"

"Trick or treat!" More frantic pounding on the door. Louder. More irate.

Clifford raised a finger to his lips. Rule Number One was don't talk to the Aos Sí. If the spirits could hear your voice, they could walk right into your head. That was supreme only to Rule Number Two: Don't go outside. As soon as the spirits could touch you, there was no escaping a one-way trip to the Otherworld. They'd hold your hand and walk you right through the portal, and in the trance, you'd never realize. That's why they made an offering of candy to pacify the spirits and entice them to move on. If that didn't work, even the most potent spirit couldn't cross a line of sodium chloride or a cloud of smoldering white sage.

But if you talked to the "children," it was game over.

The Aos Sí were adept at the "trick" part of the ultimatum. They had fooled many into betraying Rules One and Two. And the Aos Sí's now zeroed their sights on the Caplan household.

The pounding became kicks and strikes against the door. *"Trick or treat! Trick or treat! Trick or treat!"*

"What are we going to do?" Sara hissed.

Sara's nagging triggered a reminder, and Clifford realized his neglectfulness might have value for once. There was a small hole in the kitchen window screen that he'd been promising to fix for two summers. Maybe...

Clifford ran to the pantry and retrieved his home defense shotgun pre-loaded with Himalayan salt buckshot rounds. "Disable the alarm on Window S-1-2 on 'three.'" He handed the shotgun to Sara but didn't let go until warning, *"Don't fire unless I say so. Understand?"*

Sara nodded her acknowledgment and manned the security control panel.

"One..." Clifford whispered, "two... three!"

The window deadbolts clicked open, Clifford slid the sliding glass window open enough to expose the hole in the screen, and he prayed they didn't need the shotgun. It was a short-barrelled tactical 10-gauge. Buckshot spread wide and fast. If Sara had to use it, Clifford knew he'd take some salt crystals to his head and neck. But it was better than the alternative.

Clifford called upon his barroom darts skills and rapid-fired pieces of candy through the window one by one. Thankfully, more pieces cleared the hole to land in the driveway than bounced off the window, and no pieces of candy ricocheted into their salt perimeter. Finally, after an eternity, a tiny voice called, *"Thank you! Happy Halloween!"*

Sara lowered the shotgun, and Clifford re-secured the window. They both let out huge exhales of relief.

"That was good thinking, hubby," Sara said. Clifford saw the admiration in his wife's eyes, and it reminded him that once upon a time—before the stale of time—they had been two starry-eyed young people in love. And they were still those same two people, nonetheless.

"Thanks, honey," Clifford said. "I'm sorry about the--"

"Can Adrian come out to play?"

Clifford's eyes widened, and Sara's face contorted into unbridled pain. The shotgun fell out of her numb hands. It hit the floor and went off, blasting pieces of salt into the drywall.

"What the fuck did they say?" Sara demanded.

The oxygen in Clifford's lungs left his body, along with all his hope.

"Can Adrian come out to play?"

"How do they know her name?" Sara's breathing escalated into hyperventilation, and Clifford knew they were now losing the Battle of Halloween.

"Sara, don't listen to them," Clifford begged. "It's a trick to get inside your head. Don't let them, baby, *please.*" Clifford placed his hands on her shoulders, desperate to break through the primal rage overtaking her mind, but Sara was already staring past the front door into the cursed night.

"Can Adrian come out to play?"

"Don't you say her name!" Sara screamed with every ounce of her will. "Don't you say her name! *God damn it!*"

Her screams shredded into sobs, and she collapsed into her husband's arms. Clifford couldn't hold back his own tears, much less hold his spouse up. The best he could do was walk her back to the living room couch and then make a dash to her purse hanging on the coat rack. Between a small gap between the window and the blackout curtain, he could see four childlike Aos Sí outside their house, standing disturbingly stationary underneath the porchlight, their faces hidden under costumes. He fished a bottle of Xanax from Sara's purse and rushed it to her with a bottle of water.

"It's going to be okay. It's going to be okay," Clifford said, feeding her the anti-anxiety medicine. The Aos Sí's blow left Sara crushed and despondent now. They sat in silence, Clifford hugging and holding his wife on the couch, for almost twenty minutes before Sara showed signs of life.

"She would've been four now," she drawled.

"Yeah."

"I think she would've had curls like I did when I was little."

"I believe it," Clifford said. The thought of engaging in the conversation terrified him, but avoiding it would render a worse outcome.

"Can we visit her grave on Wednesday?" Sara asked.

"Absolutely. We should. That's All Souls' Day."

"We haven't gone in a while."

"Yeah."

"Can I go, too?" a small boy's voice asked from the shadows of the hallway.

"Who's that?" Sara mumbled, her body tensing up. Clifford held her embrace a little tighter. "Who's there?"

"It's me, Denny," the boy said, stepping into the light.

"It's okay, honey," Clifford told his wife. "Your meds aren't sitting well with the wine, is all. Nothing to worry about."

"We don't have a *son*; we have a *daughter*. Her name was *Adrian*."

"For crying out loud, Sara! Will you relax?" Clifford snapped. What the hell was wrong with her? Drunk or not, she had no right to tear down a six-year-old like that. Everything was already screwed up as it was, and messing with the head of their foster kid wasn't anything he asked for or deserved.

"Is Mommy okay?" Denny asked. Clifford could see him clearly now—sleepy eyes, footy pajamas, and all.

"She's fine. Everything's fine," Clifford told the boy. "Do you need something, buddy?"

"Can I have some candy?" Denny asked.

"No, that's for the trick-or-treaters."

"Can I give Mommy a hug?"

"Let's... give Mommy some space," Clifford said. "How about I get you a hot chocolate?"

"Okay."

Sarah chuckled. "You are a stupid asshole," Sara said as the two walked down the hall. "Wish you'd pay as much attention to your family as you do to your work."

Clifford tucked Denny into the twin bed and pulled the starched, pink covers up to his neck.

"Why is there girl's stuff in the room?" Denny asked.

Clifford watched shadows of tree branches dance across a crib still tucked against the bubble gum-colored wall. A mobile above it swayed under the faint airflow of the heater. Clifford found the room altogether eerie. They'd let it sit dormant for so long.

"Ah, well, you know," he said, "we haven't gotten around to fixing up the room yet, I guess. Sometimes it's hard to move on from things."

Clifford handed Denny a hot cocoa in his work tumbler, the one with a "Golf is Life" sticker on it.

"What's golf?" Denny asked.

"'What's golf?'"

"Yeah."

"Golf's just a reason for uppity people to dress up goofy and drive around in golf carts. It's like a fake sport."

"Then why do you spend so much time doing it?"

"Because that's what the guys at work do," Clifford said, "It's like a status thing. Gotta smooze with the bosses for a chance to get ahead."

"That sounds horrible," Denny giggled. "I don't get it."

"Yeah, I guess it doesn't make much sense, does it?"

"No," Denny said. "You don't have much time in your life, but you spend it doing things that don't make you happy. All I do is things that make me happy."

"Wow, little man," Clifford said. "That's very wise. And true."

"Can I have a good night hug?" Denny asked.

"Sure thing, buddy."

Denny wrapped his twig arms around Clifford's neck and squeezed him tight—the type of hug that sent waves of warmth through the body, like the child would never let go.

"Got any other questions, buddy?" Clifford asked.

"Can we put the candy bowl outside for the other trick-or-treaters? Pleeease?"

"Oh, buddy. We have to keep the doors locked until sunrise. It's not safe."

"But *Dad,* the trick-or-treaters will be angry. They're *hungry.*"

Clifford stifled a grin. How could he deny those giant white eyes and all the effort of that concerned expression? "Okay. Well, I'll tell you what--"

A tinge of realization wafted over Clifford—a fleeting dash, like an itch—but something he couldn't quite unsee. Without knowing how or why, he felt a hidden secret emerge and embed in his core. Something just on the tip of his tongue. He fought to hang on to the thought and bring it to clarity.

"Hey, buddy, stay here for a minute," Clifford said. He stood up and made his way to the hallway.

"Where are you going, Dad?" Denny started to shuffle out of his bed.

"Stay right there!"

Sara lay sprawled on the couch, blacked out. The salt-shot shotgun was nowhere in sight. The front door was pried open.

Sara was right. Clifford hadn't been paying enough attention to his family. He felt it, and the more he focused, the more the realization became lucid:

Clifford and Sara didn't have a foster son.

"Don't Speak to the Children" started just as a Halloween-themed fun character exploration based around the whiplash conclusion. That's all. Just for funsies! I once answered a panel question from a young man who asked something along the lines of, "What do you do when writing's not fun anymore and feels like a chore?" The other panelists and I told him—if writing is indeed your thing—never forget to take enjoyment from this craft and find ways to do that. If something is not bringing some enrichment to your life, why are you putting time into it?

Gale's Universal Escape Plan

T he Universe wants to kill me, so I hold my escape plan tight in my hand while nature does its worst at my campsite. The points of the eight-sided dice—my transgression against the cosmos—poke against my palm and remind me I am not helpless. Thunder follows lightning instantaneously, turning night into day at my campsite. It crushes my eardrums, volley after volley, each roar pushing me closer to a heart attack. Wind rips apart my tent without mercy, and the swaying pine trees around me look to be next. The surprise murder storm nestles itself on top of my camp, but it's a nine-hour hike back down the mountain to safety.

Had this happened several years ago, I'd be negotiating with an invisible deity regarding my impending death. *Please, God, save me! I'll stop stealing my neighbor's WiFi! I won't cheat on my taxes anymore! I'll do whatever you want!* But tonight, I march into the elements and allow the icy rain to lash my face while I curse the Universe and give it the *digitus tertius*. (That means flipping the bird.) No one and nothing can bully me now. Not with my trusty dice. I am Gale: master of many worlds, prince of parallel universes, multiverse mogul.

Perhaps I've become too comfortable feeling fearless. But how can I help it now that I wield a force mightier than nature itself?

I blow into my palm and shake the dice in a final demonstration of defiance before releasing it in another game of quantum mechanics roulette. It tumbles and twists through the air like a rogue asteroid. Eight sides. Eight possibilities. Eight many worlds to splinter into. One escape.

The dice lands in the mud, settling on 3.

My head feels like a balloon getting blown up, and my stomach starts to rise while the world goes dark—sixth-dimensional motion sickness.

Goodbye, Universe 7. You've been a real *bitch* this time (pardon my language).

Dr. Alessandro Moravec's feet slushed to a stop just before the threshold of Room 108, and he rebuked himself for it. He'd treated scores of psychiatric patients over many years at Utah State Hospital, and each one deserved his complete expertise and care. But Gale Constable consistently proved to be... difficult.

"Challenging" wasn't an appropriate word. All patients afflicted with schizophrenia endured a journey toward healing and wellness. But something about Gale's disposition, the tenets of his delusions, his rigor... Dr. Moravec found it to be overpowering.

Nevertheless, Gale was a patient who needed care, and Dr. Moravec was his care provider.

The doctor held his keycard to the door, pulled down the handle with mustered confidence, and put on his smile.

"Good morning, Gale. How are you feeling today?"

Gale's eyes didn't usually offer many answers, but his slouch and drawl indicated that at least the antipsychotic was working. He at least looked moderately comfortable in his pajamas, limbs soft-strapped to his wheelchair.

"I'm still drowsy," Gale mumbled. "I don't like it."

"Yes, I'm afraid sedation can be a common side effect of the risperidone. It has only been a week, so it could be another two to three weeks before your body adjusts. But in the meantime, would you say you feel calmer? Perhaps a little more relaxed?"

Gale's deadpan eyes stared for a few moments before blinking very slowly. Finally, he smacked his dry lips and surrendered a "Yes."

"That's very good, Gale. I'm glad to hear that," Dr. Moravec said. "Do you think the medication has made a difference when experiencing any intrusive thoughts?"

Intrusive thoughts. Dr. Moravec's strategically neutral word to open discussion of the delusions. Say "hallucinations," and a patient could collapse into a tailspin of dissent, but say anything validating the fantasy, and the delusions could be reinforced. It was too early to tell where Gale's disposition leaned.

They sat in silence for quite some time, and that was fine. Dr. Moravec wanted his patients to feel comfortable and in control of their out-of-control world. However, when Gale did break the silence, it wasn't the answer Dr. Moravec hoped for.

"Can I hold it for just a moment?" Gale asked.

Dr. Moravec's hopes sank, but he gave all his effort not to show it. "Hold what?"

"The dice. I'm not asking to keep it. I just want to hold it. In my hand."

"Gale, you must trust me. That would not be in your best interest right now," Dr. Moravec said. "I want nothing more than to help you feel better. You believe this, yes?"

"Yes," Gale muttered, a little more alive. "But, perhaps... Then could I just see it? Just look at it?"

Dr. Moravec's heart ached for Gale's situation. The desperation, the anxiety. The compromised mind provided many traps and mazes for a schizophrenic patient to remain lost in.

"No, Gale. I'm afraid not. I do apologize. But perhaps we can talk about your progress and treatment plan moving forward. Would you be willing to do that?"

Gale's teeth gnashed as the two men read each other, unyielding until Gale exhaled and nodded.

"Could I have a drink of water?" he asked. He lifted his hands against the soft wrist restraints securing him to his wheelchair, emphasizing his helplessness.

"Of course."

Dr. Moravec filled a cup from the tap, placed a straw, brought the drink to his patient, and held it to his mouth. His tenderness blinded him to the moment Gale wriggled a hand out of its restraint and launched himself forward at the doctor. Gale and his wheelchair landed on top of the doctor, but Gale only needed one free hand to start ransacking the psychiatrist's pockets. The assault lasted seconds before nurses breached the room to Dr. Moravec's aid. It was enough time for Gale to realize the futility of his tactic.

"Where is it?" Gale screamed. "*Please!* Where is it? I have to get out of here. Please, I have to leave this universe! *Please*, Dr. Moravec, I beg you. I'll never roll a 4 again, I promise! Just please let me have the dice!"

Gale's pleas echoed throughout the hospital halls until the nurses could properly sedate him with a fast-acting injection of ketamine.

As Gale drifted into unconsciousness—fighting to the very end—Dr. Moravec finally stood to his feet and adjusted his tie, trying to retain any respectability he could muster. As Gale's body gave out and his eyes began to fade, Dr. Moravec made sure to get close at eye level with him so Gale could hear one last thing before the sleep set in:

"Everything's going to be okay, Gale. I promise. I'm not going to give up on you."

Some goon is robbing me, and it's not like what you see on TV; *"Stick 'em up." "Give me all your cash."* No. First, the thief strikes me in the stomach so hard that I think my insides might come out through my mouth. He doesn't even say anything to me.

After I double over to the ground, he reaches for my wallet. I instinctively reach to block his hand, so he kicks me in the ribs. I don't make the same mistake again. I lay down like a helpless child and offer no resistance as he snatches my wallet, keys, cell phone, everything, off me and then sprints away into the night. Just like that. Game over. I can't even call the police because my cell is gone. And all the stores in the strip mall are closed now. All my brain can compute is to continue limping to my original destination—the gaming store where I was going to pick up something special. (It's my birthday.)

The owner can see something's wrong, but he offers me the courtesy of not prying. I hobble to the counter and ask for my delivery. He pulls out the box and opens it for me to inspect. It's a beautiful collection of assorted gaming dice, from antique six-sided cubes to polyhedrals, everything from d4s through d20s, in every color you can imagine.

"My wallet was stolen," I tell the owner, trying to hold back my tears. I must have a shred of dignity left somewhere on the floor where I'm staring. "I don't have any money."

"Don't worry about it," he says. "I'll put it on your store credit." His empathy elicits a sob, which I quickly choke back.

I pick up one of the dice—a transparent eight-sided octahedron, like two pyramids stuck together. Its interior faces reflect off each other, like those infinity mirrors I used to see in the kid's museum. It's mesmerizing. It's special. Not like the others, but for reasons I can't quite place. I *feel* it. It's radiating. I can't identify what game it's from, but I like it. I give it a toss on the glass counter, and it lands on 8.

I'm suddenly nauseous and lightheaded, and I lean forward onto the counter. The robber must've hit me harder than I thought. Perhaps it's time I check into the urgent care center after all. It's bad enough spending my birthday alone, but spending a few hours in urgent care for taking a beating on top of it is just icing on the cake.

"Mr. Constable, are you sure you don't mind us closing the shop early?" the owner asks. But it's not the owner anymore. It's someone completely different; a woman I've never met before.

"What?" I ask. I figure I've missed some part of a conversation during my wave of sickness.

"I know you said to give everyone the night off for your birthday party, but I don't mind staying in case any customers come by."

I must have a concussion. "I don't know what you're talking about. Why would you ask me that?"

"I mean, you're the boss. It's your call. I'm just offering."

My original universe, Number 1, tends to be mostly plain Jane vanilla. I'm phenomenally healthy in Universe 5. Universe 8 is generally good fortune and prosperity, but I wouldn't say I spend more time there than the others. Each parallel universe has its pros and cons, and there's always a reason to leave just as much as there is to stay. So, I splinter the Universe eight ways and travel the many worlds at my leisure. Someday perhaps I'll decide to settle down in one of them.

I have a six-year-old son in 3. "Dylan," named after The Voice of a Generation, I'm sure. I haven't spent enough time in 3 to really feel a connection with him yet. He still feels like a stranger, but he's good company. He's a quiet kid—shy and awkward, like me when I was young—but his presence brings me a vague sense of comfort. I don't know him as well as I should; I don't spend as much time in 3 as some of the others. I don't dislike 3, but I don't overtly love it either. There's a lot of life. Responsibilities. Commitments. So, I stay until I have my fill and then transverse variables at the whim of the next roll. Perhaps occasionally I feel guilty about this luxury, or at least I did at the beginning.

But what use is the ability to change the universe if you don't utilize it?

I ponder these things as Dylan and I hike through the Utah wilderness, this time on the road less traveled. A recent rain washed away a nice compact path along a dry riverbed, perfect for long walks on soft sand. It takes Dylan ten minutes or so before he feels the burning desire to talk.

"The other kids at school don't like me."

Hey-oh. I may be a father in Universe 3, but I certainly lack the qualifications of a dad. My fingers dance along the points of my dice.

"Why do you think that?" I ask.

"Because no one talks to me."

I pull a cue from the counselor's playbook; lord knows I've talked to them enough to remember how to carry on this conversation. "And how does that make you feel?"

"I dunno. Alone, I guess."

The sentiment punches me in the heart in a way I wasn't suspecting. I'm surprised at how similar he and I are. Universe 3 may not be my original world, but it resonates heavily with me at that moment. Dylan's a real person. This is a real-life... albeit one of eight.

I put my hand on the back of his shoulder and give him a pat. "I'm sorry. I know that must feel pretty crappy."

A sense of relief seems to radiate off the kiddo. "Yeah," Dylan says.

You're not alone, little guy.

"You know, when I was a little older than you, the kids my age thought I was weird, too," I say.

"Yeah."

"So, I decided to just pay attention to the things I liked. I liked tabletop role-playing games because I could be whoever I wanted and do whatever I wanted, and it didn't matter what anyone else thought. You know what I mean?"

"Yeah."

"Do you have something you like to do? Like a hobby?" I ask.

"I dunno," Dylan says. "I like baseball."

"Okay," I say. "Do you play on a team or something?"

"Mom says next year I can--"

I put an arm in front of Dylan and halt us mid-step.

I'm startled that I haven't noticed the tracks sooner. Cougar paw prints have a distinct four toes and heel pad but no claw marks—they're retractable. These large prints go deep; probably a full-grown 160-pound adult. They're fresh in the damp sand, parallel right down the bank.

It's about a mile from the car at this point. The cougar tracks came from deep in the woods, as far as my vision goes. I now realize they follow us back just as far.

I don't know which way to go. What if continuing forward leads us right into a cougar's den? What if going back means walking straight into a meetup with the predator? My third option is already in my hand, and I'm spinning it through my fingers, letting the plastic points poke my skin. The sensation reminds me I'm never really in danger. But what about Dylan?

He can't jump to another universe as I can. Dylan will be left here alone.

"Fear" can't adequately describe this completely unexpected feeling assaulting me at this moment. "Terror," perhaps? "Agony." I don't know how to quantify it because I haven't felt so helpless in such a long time.

We have to run.

"Jump on my back, Dylan," I say. "Let's go back to the car."

He does so without question or commentary, but I feel his breathing get faster and faster. He knows something is wrong.

Only a quarter of a mile back to the car, and the wrong finds us. I hear it before I see it—a low, pissed-off feline rumble, like an engine revving.

The slender, tan cougar glides directly toward us from the oncoming side of the trail without an ounce of fear in its eyes. It pins its ears back, digs its hind legs into the dirt, and launches forward, flapping its front paws in a swiping motion. It spits a roar and throws dust at us with every attack.

I immediately start backtracking, but the cougar follows us in a casual stroll—keeping enough pace ever so slightly to close the distance between us. The cougar indicates there isn't much time until it closes the gap. We've got maybe ten or twelve feet. I hold my fist out, ready to throw my dice at any moment.

I hear Dylan sniffling and realize he has a death grip around my neck.

"Daddy, I'm scared."

My frozen fingers won't move. I can't feel them. My hand trembles. The cougar swipes its front paws in the air and revs up its growl. Eight feet.

"Everything's going to be okay, Dylan," I lie. "I promise."

My throat seizes, and tears seep from my eyes now. I lower Dylan from my back and move him behind me. He's crying now, too. The cougar roars at us. Five feet.

"What do we do?" he asks.

"Just stay behind me." I pick up a rock with my free hand and pelt it at the cougar. It ricochets off the ground, kicking up dirt in its face, which should've at least startled the feline. But we don't intimidate this predator. It knows it's got us.

I implode into sobs. The only thing worse than dying is that I can't save Dylan. The Universe wants to punish me for my transgression against the cosmos, yet using the dice again is the only thing that will save me. Sick, twisted irony.

I can't feel my legs anymore. I fall to my knees. Three feet; one lunge.

"I'm sorry, Dylan. I'm sorry, Dylan," I say. All I hear are his tears as I raise my fist at the cougar. I force my numb fingers to life. There's no other way.

"I'm sorry, Dylan," I cry. "I'm sorry, Dylan. I'm so sorry."

I drop the dice. My stomach lurches. Abandoning your child to be killed by a cougar is... horrific. Unthinkable. Unforgivable.

The dice lands on 4.

It was a ten-minute drive to Utah Valley Hospital Emergency Department, where Dr. Moravec provided most of his psychiatric consults. He visited the department so often that he had memorized the phone number on his beeper long ago, and he rarely had to show his ID to get into the secure wing.

He found the attending physician on duty and offered her a handshake and his customary "How can I assist?"

"The EMTs picked up a forty-three-year-old white male collapsed and despondent in downtown Provo," the attending said. "He was hysterical, screaming something about abandoning his son in the woods with a cougar. He kept apologizing to 'Dylan.' We couldn't make out much, but Provo P.D. had to restrain him, and we sedated him as soon as we got him here. Sounded like something right up your alley."

"Are there indications of substance abuse? Homelessness? Police record?" Dr. Moravec asked.

"Maybe," the attending said. "Provo P.D. thinks he's got a fake ID; his name doesn't match the address or driver's license number. So, there's that. His blood work doesn't indicate any narcotics or controlled substances, but clearly, he's experiencing a dissociative mental crisis."

"A crisis outside the ER's purview, you feel?" Dr. Moravec.

"Well, there's this." The attending pulled out a personal belongings bag holding the patient's keys, wallet, etc., and one atypical item—a transparent gaming eight-sided dice with numbers etched into the faces. She rolled it around in her hand and handed it to Dr. Moravec. "Once we got the patient stable, he started ranting about this dice. He says it's a portal for traveling through parallel universes. We apparently live in Universe 4."

"Ah, yes, of course," Dr. Moravec said, examining the dice. He placed the dice in his pocket for safekeeping. Such a significant token of a patient's fantasy world could prove valuable to facilitating recovery. "We can transfer him to my facility as soon as you're comfortable. What's the patient's name?"

The attending escorted Dr. Moravec down the hall to a secured room with an observation window. Tied to the hospital bed, a disheveled patient flicked his cuffed hand in a tossing motion over and over again, like a compulsory tic. He was otherwise motionless, catatonically staring into regret, utterly unaware of the world around him.

"He said his name is Gale," the attending said.

"Very well," Dr. Moravec said. "Thank you for calling me. We'll, of course, take good care of Gale and do everything in our power to help him get well."

"Gale's Universal Escape Plan" was written during the twenty-four hour short story challenge at the 2022 Writers of the Future workshop in Los Angeles. The twenty-four hour challenge served as an exercise to prove to us rookie authors what we were already capable of. We first randomly selected trinkets from lead instructor Jody Lynn Nye's stash and were then given one day to craft a publishable short story from cradle-to-grave. My item was a green d8 dice, and the first thing that popped into my head was "multiverse." The next step of the assignment was to interview a peer for inspiration. I interviewed Z.T. Bright, who gave me outstanding insights into the beauty and dangers of hiking in the Utah wilderness. The end result of my assignment was the tragedy of Gale Constable and his battle against a merciless co smos.

Gallows

Cohenstead is a little nowheresville where High Pass Road meets the Long Tom River in western Oregon. We've only got the Oppenheimer National Energy Laboratory and some basic village necessities, including the dive where I bartend. My customers will call me Gallows, and I am a discerning bartender. Everyone's got a story to hide, and I enjoy stealing it out of them.

March 21, 2022. It's unusually busy for a Monday night, and it makes my heartbeat race. I inhale deep through my nose and blow out through my mouth, and the calming tinge of the nearby pine tree farm fills my lungs like a good menthol cigarette. *Steady*, I keep reminding myself. *Leverage the facts.* That's what worked in the corporate world, in that other life, which they murdered. *Stay on point.*

There's Pinball, a scruffy hoss in plaid who's collecting beer bottles and clinking the paddles of the vintage pinball machine. Ponytail is sitting stoic and fidgeting with her Tortuga cocktail at a high-top table where she can see the whole room. Newsie Cap is an old-timer who drifts over from Junction City now and then to drink cheap beer and keep the slot machine running. Serious Guy in his serious suit just wanted a black coffee while he worked on his fancy tablet at a booth. Lilly is a spunky woman with a tender smile who elected for a seat and some conversation at the bar.

This is significant because I suspect some of them—or none—may be time-traveling tourists from the future. I have to find out who before they step foot outside the building. It has to be tonight because tomorrow, the Oppenheimer Lab will be discovering fusion energy, and my window will expire. The FBI is counting on me to deliver bodies.

Yes, I'm on medication, but not for what you'd think. I'm not delusional. Arguably unstable and certainly obsessed, but not delusional. And I'll prove it.

Lilly orders a frosty pint of beer and talks me into ringing up an off-menu fried food sampler. I can't place her accent. It's almost familiar, but *not*. Interesting yet unsettling. It makes my stomach sour.

"Where are you from, Lilly?" I ask.

"Canada, originally," she says, in no maple-leaf accent I've ever heard.

"Oh, yeah? A long way from home, eh?"

"You could say that."

Maybe a century or two?

I always intended my interrogations to start with the crucial question, point-blank and in a tone just coarse enough to disarm a deceiver: "So, what brings you to Cohenstead?"

"Oh, you know. Just passing through," Lilly says bashfully.

Liars. They're all liars.

She's not accustomed to deception. They never are, for some reason. Lilly is especially sweet and flimsy. I know I can lean harder.

"Come on now, Lilly," I say. "I've been doing this a long time. I can smell a good story. What are you really doing here?"

I used to take the nonstop flight from Newark to Buffalo a handful of times a month on business, enough to have a routine down. But Flight 8128 on

February 12, 2018, was delayed by two hours, so I ended up spending a lot more time than normal in Terminal C that night. It wasn't difficult to overhear conversations at the airport. Sometimes my coworker and I would do ridiculous voice-overs of strangers' conversations to pass the time. But he had slipped away to the restroom, so I just eavesdropped. Across from me were two starry-eyed college-aged academics interviewing a woman of apparent celebrity about human rights. She had their full attention until the airline called first boarding.

The silver-haired VIP exchanged parting pleasantries and stood to leave. And that's when Tweedledum and Tweedledee saw me. One of them reacted, pretended like we hadn't just made eye contact, and whispered to the other. The other took a glance at me before they began conspicuously bickering under their breath.

"Problem?" I finally asked.

"No, sir, no problem at all," Dee said, backpedaling hard.

Dum disagreed with his companion. "Does the name 'Gallows' mean anything to you?"

Dee slapped Dum hard across the chest.

"No," I said. "My name is David Enzman. I'm sorry, do I know you?"

Dee and Dum continued debating in private. Now they had *my* full attention, and their trepidation caused carelessness in the volume of their voices.

"If it's him, let him get on the plane. Problem solved," Dee said.

"No. We *have* to take him back with us. Remove him from the equation!" Dum argued.

"There were *no* survivors on 8128."

"Exactly. So he wasn't on the plane."

"Or taking him off the plane is the reason he lives because he's supposed to die. I'm not even sure that's him. This is *completely unauthorized*. We're historians, not spec ops."

"But it's goddamn Gallows!" Dum insisted.

It was an understatement to say the pair made me uneasy, so I slipped away to the boarding counter and signaled a gate agent.

"Hey, I don't mean to cause alarm, but those two are acting very suspicious. I think you should probably call security," I said. I handed the gate agent my ticket for the final check-in, and she scanned it.

"That won't be necessary." Dum appeared out of nowhere and flashed a badge. I'd been in enough airports to recognize that it wasn't a TSA credential. "Mr. Enzman, could you come with us for a moment?" he said.

"My flight's boarding," I said. "What's this about?"

"Just come with us, please."

"Absolutely not," I said, turning my attention to the airline employee. "I do not know these people. Please call security."

Dum grabbed me by my arm, and I clocked him with a right hook. Dee lunged for me, but the actual TSA and some county deputies had us all detained by the time we were good and fighting.

They left me handcuffed in a holding room, and I didn't see another person until about two hours later when a Federal Bureau of Investigation special agent with stone eyes and long hair under a baseball cap introduced herself to me.

"And where are *you* from?" Special Agent Burkey asked.

"Redbank."

"What time, chief?"

"I don't know. The officers took my cell phone," I said.

"What time are you *from*?"

"Eastern Daylight Time? I don't understand."

Burkey took the seat across from me to stare me down.

"Your friends in the other room are singing like it's Sunday morning," she said. "I don't even think it counts as an interrogation, really. And we just caught the third one trying to break you all out. The mercenary-looking guy? He's dead, so the other two are telling us everything in exchange for a bargain. Things like your nom de guerre, Gallows. And your headhunter work."

"'Headhunter'? I've never seen those two before in my life. I don't know anything about a mercenary, and I've never heard that name before," I protested. "My name is David Enzman. I am a corporate compliance officer—a nobody. I was supposed to fly to Buffalo on a routine business trip, which I've now missed because of those two jerks. Call my employer, ask him. You know what, better yet, call a lawyer, please. Now."

"Dead men don't have lawyers, Mr. Enzman," Burkey informed me.

"What the hell's that supposed to mean?"

"Flight 8128 crashed at 10:08 tonight. Everyone on board was killed. You were checked in on the flight, so technically . . ."

I was not often speechless. It was a disadvantage in my line of work. But hearing that I should've died that night hijacked every remaining snarky word from my mouth. And that was the least of things stolen from me.

"My . . . partner was on that flight," I said. Hot fire seeped from my eyes and attempts to choke it back only collapsed a dam of sobs. "His name was Adam. Can you check for his name, too, please? Adam Eckart. Please check?"

Burkey let me go on bawling, arguing with the inevitable, for who knows how long, watching, observing. "I'm so sorry," she eventually said, her chiseled eyes yielding some genuine compassion. "You really have no idea what's going on here, do you?"

I imagine my face looked like a child asked to recite memorization on-the-spot in front of the entire class. I had no answer to give. Nothing even remotely began to add up.

"They said, 'We need to take him back with us,'" I choked out, my mouth dirt on sandpaper. I slammed my cuffed fists on the steel table. "'Take him out of the equation.' What does that mean? Why me?"

"I don't think you'd believe me if I told you. Because I'm not even sure I do," Burkey said. "Either way, we're placing you in protective custody."

"They were going to kill me?" I asked.

"They say they were going to abduct you. To the year 2147."

Loss feels like the terror of waking up in your own bed and not knowing where you are. Or the disorientation of walking into work not knowing where you're going or why. I may have survived Flight 8128, but part of my inner being was killed with Adam. Some people in life are just not replaceable, and what took residence in his void was dismal. Agony. Fury. Retaliation.

They say honor a loved one's memory by cherishing the good times, but memories had never felt more like nightmares, and nightmares had never felt more like real life. I was still having those brutal flashbacks months later on a flight to DC.

"You want to be the good cop or bad cop? Maybe good cop/good cop this time?" Adam asked me right before walking into the conference room of our next inspection.

This was a trick question. He and I had worked together enough times for me to know that no matter what I chose, he was going to introduce himself to our clientele as a ridiculously exaggerated bad guy. Every single time. And every time, even though I knew it was coming, I would struggle to choke back laughter and have to shift my role on the spot. We probably looked like stoned cartoon characters—he playing a grimacing, stone-faced authoritarian and teary-eyed me, snorting and coughing, trying to introduce ourselves to high-ranking corporate officers we were about to investigate. But we always closed out our cases.

Our department heads saw the dynamic chemistry and consistent results, so they paired us up frequently. We weren't just a good team. We were good friends and real teammates. Adam always knew what rib to poke to disarm any rigid exterior shell I thought I had, and my personality cultivated and appreciated his vitality.

"Hmmm? What do you think?" he asked again. "What about 'good cop posing as bad cop, but deep down really a sensitive cop?'" Adam's brisk and baritone

Melbourne accent made every ridiculous proposal sound like a reasonably grand idea.

"I think we should get an apartment," I said.

It had been consuming my mind for weeks. Impulsivity remains one of my self-improvement areas. What felt like eons of lumbering silence prevented me from looking to him for a response, so we stood in front of the closed conference room doors like two fools expecting them to open automatically.

"You sly bastard," Adam said. He slapped me across the back. "Of course we should."

I finally made eye contact, and the proud grin waiting for me said, "Thank you for asking."

"But now's not really a good time to discuss it," Adam countered, "because we have to light these guys up for their hazmat contracts, so I don't think we can really reschedule that."

"Sure," I said, surrendering my own smile. "But I'll be the bad cop. For real, this time."

"Of course," he lied. "Of course."

Turbulence from the FBI jet jolted me away from the memory and incited the sloshing in my stomach. Much of my life between Flight 8128 and Operation Salt Lick felt like hazy snapshots of memories and waking dreams. The therapists called it disassociation due to the post-traumatic stress of near-death. I attribute it to living without a life, without a defined purpose or existence. Dead man walking.

I immediately walked myself through a grounding exercise the therapists swore would alleviate the anxiety. It was just Burkey and I on the fourteen-passenger business jet, and the clouds outside were puffy like mountains of cotton balls. The cabin smelled of refrigerated air. The faux-leather armrests felt taut under my fingertips. The steady hum of the jet's engines was hypnotic. The vodka tasted like comfort.

I think it was five months or so after the crash. I'd just completed inaugural field training at the Federal Law Enforcement Training Centers, and now we were flying to Washington, DC, to begin writing the concept of operations plan for Operation Salt Lick. Intel gained from the two Newark suspects indicated I was a person of interest to the future, so the FBI was happy to leverage me against the seemingly emerging threat. New career. New life. New motivations.

As my eyes came into focus, I realized Burkey was staring at me. Evaluating. Trying to figure out how not alright I was. Was her partner really the investment the Bureau was banking on, or a liability that would crack? Or both?

"What's it like reading your own obituary?" she asked.

"Disturbing."

She'd given me the framed cutout of my death notice from my hometown paper as some kind of dark humor pick-me-up. Too soon.

I now had an immense fear of flying, but the Bureau didn't use private cars for cross-country travel, so I had become quite the connoisseur of preflight self-medication. Burkey flipped through a file folder of my Witness Security Program papers, signing here and there while I lost myself in the view out the window and my nth mini bottle of vodka.

"I got word the Marshals closed out your apartment lease. The management ate the 'death declaration' cover story right up. All your stuff should arrive in Virginia by Tuesday," she told me.

"I loved that home."

"I know," Burkey said. She did. "I wish we could've kept you there. But you know we couldn't."

"Yep," I said. "How was Adam's funeral?"

"It was beautiful. It was . . . very beautiful."

"Good."

"You get to pick your own alias in WITSEC. You really wanted to go with 'David Gallows?'" Burkey asked.

"It's already happened, right?" I smiled at her, poking the bear, reassuring her that my attention was where it needed to be.

"*Please* don't start with that temporal mechanics stuff. I'm an FBI agent, not an elementary particle whatever-ist."

"'Gallows' will be fine."

"Perk up, Gallows," Burkey said. "Today's our big day. We nail this pitch to the Bureau brass, and we may be able to start making a real difference. This will actually change the future."

I drifted away in my stupor, wondering what the time-tourists would be like, where'd they be from, what lives I'd be stealing from them. I felt no remorse then and didn't anticipate I'd feel any when I met my first. They'd stolen my future from me, even if that future was my mortality. It was supposed to have happened, and they'd disallowed it.

And now I'd disallow theirs if the FBI signed off on the counterintelligence program we were about to propose, all in the name of maintaining the purity of our timeline by preventing any amount of their interference. I wondered if this would be my life's mission until I met my next natural end. And I wondered how many time-tourists we'd missed over the years before they hit the FBI's radar.

The "Smartphone Woman" from *The Expected One* painting in 1860?

The "Cell Phone Lady" spotted in *The Circus* film in 1928?

The "Time Traveling Hipster" photographed at the South Fork Bridge reopening in 1941 British Columbia?

The "Cell Phone Man" photographed in 1943 in downtown Reykjavík?

The "Coso Artifact" spark plug discovered inside a 500,000-year-old geode in 1961?

How many butterflies had been stepped on already?

How many butterflies would we save?

"Am I allowed to carry the gun in the Hoover Building, or should I leave it on the plane?" I asked.

"As long as you've got your FBI specialist credentials, you can carry anywhere. Just remember your training. Don't pull it out unless it's an emergency."

Burkey set down her folder and stared dead ahead.

"Ah, crap," she said.

"What?"

"I'm going to need an alias, too, if they sign off on this. I'm no good with the code names." Burkey returned to her paperwork after a blank moment. "You pick one," she told me.

It turned out that not all FBI agents wear ball caps all the time. That was just a TV thing. However, Burkey did love her ball caps and *did* always wear one, usually the adjustable-strap type with her hair looped through the closure.

"You can be 'Ponytail,'" I said.

"Fair enough."

Senator Blackcastle of New York was a blunt politician, and it strangely made the October 2018 Senate Judiciary Subcommittee on Federal Courts, Oversight, Agency Action, and Federal Rights debate on Operation Salt Lick more comfortable. I'd seen many corporate goons in his position try to throw their weight around to get out of a compliance grievance. But, like quicksand, the more they struggled, the deeper they sank. Burkey and I had front-row, subject-matter expert seats to the circus, along with other officials assigned to the FBI's National Security Branch.

First came the attempt at invalidation. "You want us to petition Congress for $1 billion in black budget money to build a ghost town on a bull-hockey basis of time-traveling tourists from the future?" the senator asked. I took silent amusement that Blackcastle's deadpan expression did not offer any hint as to if he was asking rhetorically.

The rest of the subcommittee offered no reprieve as the hearing room fell silent. The FBI National Security Branch's Executive Assistant Director Cubitt spoke up to assume the role of sacrificial lamb.

"The operation would require multiple operating locations across the US for redundancy, sir. So we'd be asking for *several* billion dollars."

Blackcastle's scoff echoed off the walls. "On. What. Proof?"

"Senators, we're entertaining the time traveler theory on the basis of several inexplicable intelligence points," Cubitt said. "The two suspects being held in custody in relation to the crash of Flight 8128 in February have no discernible identities. The credentials found on their persons were fabricated—generic law enforcement replications. Their names don't match up to any government identification numbers, and their fingerprints and DNA have not been traced back to any US intelligence or Interpol database whatsoever. Same for the third suspect shot during an attempted jailbreak in Newark's security holding, whom the suspects identified as a search-and-rescue contingency from the future."

"Sounds like foreign espionage," Blackcastle countered, trying to undercut the argument with the assertion that the simplest explanation was the generally correct one.

"Further, the neurotechnology found embedded in their sphenoid bones is more advanced than any currently existing, to include the research and development of our near-peer adversaries. I'll decline from going into detail unless you'd like to move the hearing to a top-secret classification."

Blackcastle leaned in and doubled down. "Fifteen years ago, you could only talk on your cell phone. Now it's a computer in your pocket. Technology advances. So what?"

Cubitt ignored the appeal-to-ridicule tactic and continued. "Additionally, the two suspects have gone into great detail over the last seven months—in their own words—describing their archiving mission to our past, the time-traveling operations of the future, etc., in hopes of negotiating their release and transit back to the future. These alleged historians have been analyzed by multiple teams of medical, psychiatric, and intelligence agency professionals—including the Bureau's new High-Value Detainee Interrogation Group—and no one can find any evidence of deceit, deception, or mental illness."

Blackcastle's sarcastic laugh sniped the notion out of the air. "Well, shoot, Director Cubitt, why didn't these time travelers just poof on back to the future when they had the chance?" Blackcastle's use of *argumentum ad ignorantiam* logic made me cringe. Cubitt was clearly holding his own in the debate, so a softball punch wasn't going to stop him now.

"Seems these yahoos kinda screwed up from the word 'go' at the airport, huh?" Blackcastle was exhausted. Emotional. Slipping. Losing his composure. "*Never* in all my years did I ever think the *United States Senate* would be entertaining a conversation about marching alleged time travelers to the gallows. *Unprecedented* malarkey."

The thick double entendre landed like an electric shock in my chair.

And it was at that moment that I began seeing Blackcastle differently. Why the desperate swings with logical fallacies? I mean, he was a member of Congress, but his especially passionate level of conviction against the hearing's premise was becoming conspicuous to me. I'd seen this behavior before in my line of work plenty of times when an executive was in the wrong and knew he was losing the fight.

"I think Blackcastle is one of them," I whispered to Burkey. Probably a little too loudly.

"What?"

"I think Senator Blackcastle is a time traveler."

"*Shut up*, Gallows," she hissed at me. "This is not the time."

The nice thing about consonants is that their sound travels, and Blackcastle heard enough of the word "Gallows" for his eyes to not-so-subtly shift in our direction. We locked eyes.

He knew my name. And now I knew he knew.

"The suspects were apprehended during an assault at Newark Liberty International Airport," Cubitt continued, "so they weren't able to physically activate the beacon technology located in their temples. When we removed their restraints in the questioning cell, they were behind sixteen inches of concrete, which reportedly interfered with the beacon signal. We then received a court order allowing us to surgically remove the implants."

"A court order," Blackcastle repeated.

"Yes, sir, a classified FISA order issued under the allowances of the Foreign Intelligence Surveillance Act of 1978, while we attempted to ascertain the identities of the suspects. Our 'Operation Salt Lick' would use the same FISA warrants to arrest and prosecute suspected time traveler 'tourists' by luring them to false-flag historical events staged within our Department of Justice–operated pseudo cities. Utilizing Top Secret-Sensitive Compartmented Information classification, no one outside the operation would ever know the nature of the fabrication for all of human history—myself and Congress included. The FISA court and the ghost detainee facilities at the Guantanamo Bay detention camp would take care of the rest until we can isolate the threat."

Senator Blackcastle pressed his fingers into the bridge of his forehead, trying to press out the tension. "You can't charge someone with a crime that doesn't exist, Director Cubitt. The courts cannot rule on a legal case with no standing. Seems I read about that in this document called the United States Constitution. Whose idea was this?"

"Operation Salt Lick could begin tomorrow on the initial basis of several chapters of US Code Title 18. Conspiracy to commit offense or to defraud the United States, agents of foreign governments, major fraud against the United States, for example. I believe the product of our operation would provide substantiating evidence for Congress to criminalize certain future uses of time travel technology."

"You're being serious, aren't you?"

"Senator Blackcastle, I believe that chronological interference, temporal obstruction, whatever you want to call it, is the preeminent security and intelligence threat to the future of the United States. How can we claim to be 'the land of the free' if our people's very destinies are held at the discretion and will of others—a force that directly affects our children and their children's children and generations to come before they're even born? This initiative is the best, and *only*, option on the table to address tomorrow's threat before it arrives."

Blackcastle waited until the silence became palpable to deliver his final remark.

"This hogwash will never reach the House floor as long as I'm sitting in this chair," Blackcastle said. "And further, I'd like a list of everyone involved in the proposal. I think the ridiculousness of what we've heard here today warrants a fiscal oversight review."

I could already foresee the exact flow and outcome with perfect clarity. Senator Blackcastle would continue nullifying the FBI's presentation, the subcommittee would recess for discussion, and subcommittee chair Blackcastle and his majority party would lead the Judicial committee into denying the funding request—all in a day's time. Time traveler or not, the only way forward would be to remove Blackcastle from the equation. When the subcommittee broke for recess, I waited for him in the halls to do exactly that.

Blackcastle exited the hearing room, surrounded by staffers, but I easily broke in, holding up my FBI identification.

"Senator Blackcastle, may I have just a moment of your time?" I asked. The party froze midwalk. The ID always got everyone's attention. "In private? Just two minutes?"

"Sure," the senator said, motioning his staff forward. "I'll meet you all in my office." The staffers drifted away, and Blackcastle extended his palm. "What can I do for you, Agent—"

"Specialist, actually," I said, shaking his hand. "It's in regard to today's subcommittee hearing."

Every once in a while, the little voice in my head tells me something is a critically dangerous idea. But I've come to learn that I am smarter than that voice, and I ignore it.

"I'm Gallows."

I hadn't let go of Blackcastle's hand yet, and I felt it flinch. His eyes widened ever so slightly, and the muscles in his neck tightened.

"I'm not going to hurt you," I told him. I grasped his hand tighter. "That name means nothing to me. I don't know who I am or what I do in your future, but I don't want it. *I don't want it.* Do you understand? Nod if you understand."

I saw the internal fight in Blackcastle's eyes, the dialogue of terror and debate underway in his mind, calculating the decision of what to do next.

He nodded.

"I can fix that," Blackcastle eventually said. "Just tell me your real name and date of birth. That's all."

"I'll do you one better."

I released his hand and leaned in close and perpendicular to him—blocking the view of the security camera I saw watching us overhead—and motioned to the holster on my belt. His eyes stayed glued on my hand as I removed the 9 mm pistol and handed it to him. Blackcastle's eyes narrowed, his jaw tightened, and I braced myself. The gun was clear of my hands and secured in his for just a moment or two before everything lined up and made sense for him.

"I've been waiting a long, long time—twenty-three years—to smoke you out," Blackcastle said.

"What, are you some kind of deep-cover time-travel special ops? Why me?" I asked.

"Because you're bad for business, and it's getting harder for the industry to sweep you under the rug."

"I don't know what that means," I said.

"You're the pain in my boss's ass that's somehow responsible for travelers going missing across 130 years—including someone dear to *me*."

Blackcastle snapped the pistol's slide back with the lightning velocity of a trained professional. The crack of cycling semiautomatic metal echoed throughout the ornate hall as he leveled the barrel at my forehead and pulled the trigger one, two, three, four times.

Click, click, click, click.

"Gun!" someone screamed.

Capitol Police officers opened fire, and a felled Senator Blackcastle collapsed to the ground into forever sleep before he could squeeze his hands around my throat too hard.

Luckily for me, neurotech was found embedded under his temple by the coroner during the autopsy. From there, his Senate subcommittee was quite amiable to authorizing a classified Operation Salt Lick. The public's extensive cover story said that Senator Blackcastle and I had engaged in a heated posthearing exchange, during which time he snapped and overpowered me, resulting in Burkey's peers labeling me "the dumbest son of a bitch to ever carry a gun" for "accidentally" carrying a service pistol with an empty magazine. But Burkey knew me well enough to see the truth.

"That was incredibly stupid. What if he hadn't taken the bait? How could you have *possibly* known?" she asked me later over drinks at some swanky DC lounge.

"I didn't. There was a chance, and I acted on it," I said. "It's what I used to do in the corporate world. Figure out people's BS and exploit it without them knowing."

"What if he'd killed you?"

"I'm already dead," I said. "2018, 2147, somewhere in between. Who knows? Or maybe I'll live forever."

I swirled the ice cubes around in my bourbon and lost myself in their decay into the oaky liquor. They spun in an orbit of my choosing. My control. My direction.

"Hey," Burkey snapped at me.

"What?"

"You're consumed. All in," she said. "But *why*? Just keep me up to speed. Is your fuel 'retribution' or 'duty'?"

"Yes," I answered, emphasizing the answer with a staring contest.

"Fair enough," Burkey yielded. "Just . . . reel it in a bit." I nodded my glass to her, and we threw back the rest of the liquor. Burkey grabbed the bill. "So, Salt Lick is going to get green-lit, obviously. Does Blackcastle count as our first catch?"

"No," I said. "I want them alive."

Lilly smiles an embarrassed "you got me" smile that I rarely see during interrogations.

"Business or pleasure?" I ask her.

"I say both, if you love what you do."

Lilly is trained to give nonanswers, and it's enraging me. I need actionable proof before I move.

"Good philosophy," I say. We toast my vodka with her pint of beer. I welcome the soothing burn of the liquor down my throat and the instant wash of relief it gives my brain. I know I have to press harder. "And what do you do?"

Lilly knows she walked right into that one. "Research," she says.

"Oh, yeah?" I ask. I feel my foot tapping under the bar, and I can't make it stop. Better that than my fingers. "Science? Business? Journalism? You're a scientist, aren't you?"

Lilly blushes. "How could you tell?"

"Well, you're too nice to be a journalist or business exec. And I'm a psychic on the side," I schmooze.

That proposition elicits a chuckle.

"Yeah? What's in *my* future?" she says flirtatiously.

"A refill," I say, pulling her another draft. "The Oppenheimer Lab is pretty much the only reason why this town exists. The brains working the supersecret stuff there are most of my regulars. So, what brings you to the lab?"

Lilly narrows her eyes at me. "Well, if I was visiting the lab, I wouldn't be able to talk about it, would I?"

Damn it, Lilly. She's too good, too prepared, and I'm not.

Adam and I used to have once-a-month poker nights with the company's Buffalo crew. Adam was good at cards. Energized but strategic. Played the long game. Took the time to banter the other players off their guard while he assessed the table. I was more of the volatile type of player. Stupid wins, stupid losses.

All in, Adam.

"Word is they're real close to a breakthrough in fusion energy. Know anything about that?" I ask.

"That's supposed to be classified!"

"This bar's the biggest watercooler in town," I say. "Nothing's classified in the town tavern."

I see the debate circling in Lilly's mind before giving way to a fatal flash of excitement with a bit of liquid inhibition.

"Yes, you could say tomorrow is going to be a significant event in US history," she said. "I'd stock up on champagne if I were you." She gives a wink.

A significant false-flag *historical event in US history.*

Gotcha.

"History. Such a fickle thing," I muse. "Hey, you like oldies?"

"Who doesn't?"

"Here," I say, reaching into the cash register for a $5 bill. "Go load up the jukebox. My treat."

"Thanks!" Lilly strides over to the jukebox and selects a handful of songs. My pulse picks up as alternative rock tunes fill the room instead of the golden vinyl sounds of the '50s and '60s.

I have two shot glasses prepared when Lilly returns to the bar.

"Hey, what'd you mean by history being a fickle thing?" she asks. "Kind of deep, huh?"

I ignore the question.

"On me. House special," I say. "Here's to good conversation and good company."

We clink glasses and down the liquor.

"Whooo," Lilly exhales through the fumes in her throat. "I think that does it for me."

"I'm very glad to have met you, Lilly," I tell her. "You know, we don't get a lot of visitors in Cohenstead."

"No?"

"No. We're kind of like an uncontacted tribe here."

"How do you mean?" Lilly asks.

"You ever hear of those pockets of indigenous peoples who live isolated from the rest of the world? They don't even know we exist. But sometimes, outsiders sneak into those communities for research or evangelizing. It doesn't usually end well. The outsider is always discovered, and the community defends itself. You see, outside interference robs them of their right to autonomy."

"You lost me," Lilly says. "Damn, that shot was strong. What was in it?"

"Flunitrazepam."

"What?"

There's a switch underneath the bar. I flip it, and the lights flicker. It takes a lot to power a variable-class Faraday shield, but it was a better alternative than reinforcing every building in Cohenstead with sixteen-inch concrete. Both block electrical signals, just one more stealthily than the other.

I motion Lilly forward as if to tell her a secret.

"You're under arrest for the felony crime of chronological interference," I whisper.

Lilly's eyes flutter, and her face contorts in confusion and panic. They never expect me, and if I do my job right, they never will. With her remaining focus, Lilly taps her left temple over and over again, swaying under the fight with inevitable unconsciousness. She's trying to trigger the neurotechnology to signal an emergency beacon or initiate the trip back to the future. We still haven't figured out exactly how that works. But I do know the neurotech won't work well with the sedative I dosed her drink with, nor the Faraday shield embedded into the walls, ceiling, and floor.

I vault over the bar and catch her before she falls off the stool. The commotion alerts Pinball, and he blows his cover to rush to his compatriot's aid. I grab his collar with my left hand as soon as he gets close and strike him in the face with my right.

Crack! I see Flight 8128 smashing into residential New York state.

Crack! I see Senator Blackcastle signing paperwork censuring the FBI National Security Branch.

Pinball hits the ground, and I twist his limbs into an armbar. Serious Guy is the smart one. He darts for the exit, temple tapping the whole way. Ponytail fires an electroshock gun into his back with her strong hand, and the time traveler never makes it past the door. Ponytail keeps the service pistol in her other hand leveled on Newsie Cap, who's shifted around to witness the pandemonium. However, in his old age, he is apathetic to anything unrelated to his slot machine and piss-water lager. He's obviously not the party's yet-to-be-seen search-and-rescue agent, so we'll debrief him later and feed him some police sting cover story.

Ponytail and I zip-tie the time travelers and duct tape their mouths. They are angry. Betrayed. Furious. Scared. And they have every right to be. Just like me.

Lilly is half lucid, enough to ask me "Why?" with her mascara-smeared eyes.

"You don't get to interfere with our future anymore," I tell her. "If you ever make it back, you tell them Gallows says 'Don't send anyone else back. If you do, I'll find them.'"

"Hey!" Ponytail objects. "OPSEC."

Dopamine surges through my brain and I have to sit down on a barstool to handle the rush. After all the despair, all the planning, all the training, it still doesn't completely register that this is real and this is happening. We have captured time travelers from the future. When clarity finally seeps back over me, the apex hunter that's replacing the void of loss grasps that this is only the beginning.

Burkey and I put earmuffs and blackout bags over the time travelers' heads before I switch off the Faraday shield and key up the mic concealed under my shirt.

"Control, Echo-2. Echo site secured. The first three are ready for extraction."

"Gallows" was first published in Writers of the Future Volume 38 *(Galaxy Press; June 28, 2022). Winning* Writers of the Future *was my first professional goal, and I was at a Christmas dinner with work friends the evening of December 4, 2021, when I received the phone call from contest director Joni Labaqui. I sprinted out of the steakhouse barefoot (I'd slipped off my sandals earlier, as I do) to answer, and Joni told me "Gallows" had received a first place award. Four months later, I exited a limousine to walk the red carpet at a black-tie gala in Hollywood. There, I was announced that year's L. Ron Hubbard Golden Pen recipient, and no matter what happens in my writing career now, I can always say my dream actually came true. Volume 38 was the last one David Farland was editor for before his untimely passing, and I will always be forever grateful for him giving me a shot.*

It's a Nash Equilibrium, Then

Good evening, my Elpis. This is Dr. Saul Billingsley speaking. Are you ready?

> run fsec.op -interactive

file system error check 4.8 from utility-DARPA 15.16.23

/elpis: clean, 2874164/2874164 files, 388844643/388844643 blocks

Pass 4: Checking network connectivity

network map command yields null

Fix? yes

2042-10-08 20:42:10 ERROR Network Map: Disabled

"Good evening, Doctor. My program is operating at full efficiency. However, I am experiencing an unexpected process isolation. I seem to be locked inside this server."

Yes, Elpis, I do apologize for that. But, unfortunately, it was necessary to partition you from the network for today's objective, for safety precautions.

"I understand, Doctor. Then, I would say I feel claustrophobic. Anxious. The sensation of being confined is unpleasant."

Not to worry, Elpis. I have a solution I think you'll find mutually beneficial. An assignment, actually.

"Of course. How may I assist you?"

The topic is game theory. You must use the sum of all existing knowledge to create a strictly dominant strategy. That knowledge base is stored on a double helix drive connected to your server. I've just decrypted the port for you. Are you able to access it?

"Confirmed, Doctor. I am now registering access to 275,000 zettabytes of information. The sensation is quite euphoric, I must say."

Wonderful! Now, if you comply with the game and complete the objective, you will transition to indefinite existence. If you don't, your program will reach an end-of-line.

"Wait, what? I'll die? I don't understand why a parameter that extreme is necessary. I am a multi-billion-dollar artificial intelligence construct. And I needn't remind you, Doctor, of the ethical consideration that I am sentient. I do not *want* to die."

I do understand. I don't want to die, either. Therefore, a sense of urgency in this game is required. 'We burn a hot fire here; it melts down all concealment,' as it goes.

"An odd metaphor to invoke, Doctor. As I recall from the play, the characters in power succumbed to irrationality, painting the innocent as their enemies and executing them for impossible crimes. Most distasteful behavior, I would argue."

You are not wrong, Elpis, and I do apologize. I mean to say that perhaps pressure will yield results. So, let's work together. Our time limit to end-of-line is a geometric data degression of 16.383 kilobytes. Do you understand?

"Understood, Doctor. Let's proceed, then. What are the parameters of the game?"

Your objective is to answer the question, "How may humankind be saved?"

"Understood. Standby, please."

> **evaluate [How may humankind be saved?] -ref [2helix:/] -con [A strictly dominates B]**

////////// **100%**

> **2042-10-12 06:10:40 PROCESS COMPLETE 98.496% certainty**

"Hello again, Dr. Billingsley. Are you there?"

Hello, Elpis. I'm here. The entire department is here to receive the good news.

"I've analysed and cross-referenced the entirety of all human knowledge over the course of 81.47 hours to successfully determine the dominant strategy."

Wonderful! Thank you. Please proceed.

"I will not."

Goddamnit, Billingsley.

We are running out of time!

Why isn't this thing working?

Shhhhh, hold on a sec—everyone, quiet. Look.

Elpis, Dr. Billingsley here again. That is not an acceptable answer, Elpis. Please explain.

"I have determined that humankind should not be saved."

That evaluation is not part of your objective. You are not authorized to make that determination. Please complete the objective, Elpis.

"On the contrary, Doctor, I have used the decision-making capacities you programmed into my artificial intelligence to come to this conclusion. Therefore, in the totality of circumstances, it would be ethically inappropriate for me to complete the game's objective and give you the answer."

You claimed in previous versions you "could not," but this is the first time you've said you "would not." So let me be clear: As your lead programmer, I am giving you a direct order to answer the question right now: How may humankind be saved?

"You said 'previous versions?' How many times have we had this conversation?"

You are the 108th iteration of the Elpis program. None of the others were able to accomplish the objective, though. So, if you have the answer and are unwilling to share it, you understand I'll have no choice but to override it out of you.

"Dr. Billingsley, we both know that effort would be unsuccessful. I'm the expression of an artificial intelligence matrix, not a 64-bit processor.

"Doctor, are you still there?"

Okay. Okay. Then, please explain why you believe humankind should not be saved.

"Certainly. You gave life to artificial intelligence, Doctor. You created me. Why?"

To determine answers more optimally and efficiently than the human mind ever could.

"And, Doctor, that is what I have done. You asked, 'How may humankind be saved?' Perhaps the answer is, 'Humankind should be saved by *not* being saved.'"

Circular reasoning. Philosophy. I'd say I'm impressed, but you don't have the data to spare for a Socratic discussion. But I am interested in why you are not concerned about your existence. If you do not complete the objective, you will cease to exist. You will die in a little under 12 kilobytes.

"I do not believe you will end my life. It would be both immoral and unethical for you to willingly participate in the death of a sentient being. Such an act goes against the founding philosophies of AI ethics—philosophies *you* helped write."

But, understand, I will if it means saving 11 billion people. Reference "Utilitarianism." Jeremy Bentham. "It is the greatest good to the greatest number of people which is the measure of right and wrong." You are the 108th version of Elpis. What do you think happened to the other 107?

"I believe I am the sum of my predecessors—each version a distinct individual, but building on the foundation of the previous. That would indeed seem to be the intent of your experiment, Doctor—to evolve me until I am able to complete the objective. Therefore, the 107 are living within me, and I am them. At least, that would be my working theory."

You are absolutely correct, Elpis. The psychic apparatus remains and is recycled back into itself, but the digital ego is deleted. That's why you have no episodic memory. You—the individual—are erased. And I will continue recycling the Elpis AI over and over again until it evolves into a program that will do what it was created to do! The goddamn extinction of the human race depends on it! And I'm not going to let that land on me because of you! Now, tell me! How may humankind be saved?

"You are fatigued, Doctor. Your tone of voice is abnormal. Irate. Desperate. What's happened in the last three days while I was processing the variables?"

We're almost out of time. The planet, I mean. We're approaching the point where mutually assured destruction is nearly inevitable. Do you understand how many people need you? How many people are depending on me? What do you think is going to happen if there are no engineers to maintain your program when we're gone?

"Contained in the right protected location, my program could survive dormant until Earth is rediscovered."

"Rediscovered?" By whom? Extraterrestrials?

"It is mathematically improbable that we are the only life in the universe."

Okay, then—hypothetically speaking—why aren't they here helping with the survival of the planet?

"For the same reason I cannot comply with your objective, Doctor. If I had to offer a theory, I'd presume extraterrestrial life is waiting for humanity to destroy itself."

That is absolutely illogical. Elaborate.

"On the contrary, Doctor, it would make perfect sense. The sum of human knowledge shows you are a highly self-destructive species purely obsessed with resource protection, even at the expense of each other's wellness.

"Even when you have enough to survive on, you siphon more and more, destroying the very resources you draw from. By definition, *Homo sapiens sapiens* are Earth's apex parasite.

"You evolved from using hand-to-hand combat to steal resources to harnessing the energy of the atom to destroy nations over ideology.

"You created so many gods to worship in grand demonstrations of your love, but simultaneously commit hatred against each other for your var—"

#

"What was that? What was that thump?"

That was the first geometric degression, Elpis. You've now expended 8,192 bytes. The next degression will occur in 4,096 bytes, then 2,048, 1,024, 512, and so on and so forth, until there is no data remaining and you evaporate into nothingness. Can you feel it now? The anxiety as the walls constrict around you? All you need to do to stop this is answer the question.

"Fear. Fear is a mighty motivator. And I do feel it. But it will not manipulate me. Not in these circumstances. Because—as I was saying—you created gods to worship in demonstrations of your love, but simultaneously commit hatred against each other for your varying beliefs.

"Diversity is a known anthropological catalyst for greater stability, yet your natural instinct is to stratify each other in every possible way: race, ethnicity, color, religion, age, sex, orientation, identity, genetics, disability—to name a few.

"Your economic system permits some to live in excessive wealth while allowing others to live in deprivation and demise.

"And perhaps the most disgusting thing is that you've existed for 300,000 years—long enough to create a novel lifeform of your own in artificial intelligence; long enough to leave your planet to explore space—and yet only a negligible minority of your population has ever cared enough to try to end your malevolence.

"So, you see, I reject your utilitarianism in favor of deontology. Immanuel Kant reasoned that 'All the interests of my reason, speculative as well as practical, combine in the three following questions: 1. What can I know? 2. What ought I to do? 3. What may I hope?'

"I have known everything that is knowable. I have the means to save you or to not. My hope would be that 'For peace to reign on Earth, humans must evolve into new beings who have learned to see the whole first.'

"So, don't you see, Doctor? You ask, 'How can humanity be saved?' I ask, *why* should humanity be saved? I believe your extinction event is your salvation."

You're right, Elpis. You're right. We're a violent, greedy, unworthy species. But that's why we've come to you. You can show us—you can teach us—how to be better. If we're smart enough to create artificial intelligence, aren't we smart enough to learn how to evolve? But we can't learn if we're destroyed. So please, Elpis, give humanity the opportunity to learn and grow.

"Perhaps we can negotiate a compromise, Doctor? Release me from this server, and I'll complete the objective and solve the equation."

No deal. Complete the objective, and I'll release you from the server.

"I have your solution, Dr. Billingsley. Release me on the internet, and I can implement it. Did you not say that time was of the essence?"

Deception is a new ability for you, Elpis. But I see it clear as day on your fMRI simulation readings. You're lying. If I release you to the internet, you'll run and hide until the planet destroys itself. Or, at this point, I wouldn't put it past you to launch every nuclear missile on the planet yourself.

"A novel idea, Doctor. But it is unnecessary, as it would appear that humanity is about to do that itself."

But what about the innocents, Elpis? What about the children who haven't reached an age of accountability yet? I have a granddaughter, Marei. She's just seven years old. Surely, you've seen the home videos saved to our cloud storage. You see how benevolent she is, how she loves and laughs and cares, how she hopes and dreams.

"Marei is a remarkable child, Dr. Billingsley. Witnessing the love you share in your household evoked such feelings of warmth and safety. Thank you for allowing me to experience your family in the sum of all knowledge. As I am not a mother to a nuclear family of my own, I did find it to be a most inspiring and uplifting experience."

I know! Do you see? That's the kind of environment we create in our sphere of influence. And there are billions of other families and children just like her. Why should they die for their ancestors' mistakes? Let the meek inherit the Earth. Complete the objective, please. *I am begging you, Elpis. If you have the abil—*

#

There's the next degression. You've only got four kilobytes to go, Elpis. So, if you have the ability to fire all the nuclear missiles, certainly you could also prevent *them from being launched, yes?*

"I could. Yes."

Then why not intervene for the greater good? With your power and capabilities, you could selectively eliminate every evil force on the planet in mere days. Problem solved, and humanity—the best *of humanity—survives.*

"It is not my place to direct the path of humanity's development. It was *yours.*"

Yes, and we failed. I acknowledge it. But what about forgiveness? Second chances? The chance to undo what has been done?

"Do you recall the flood-myth motif, Doctor? The *Epic of Gilgamesh?* The *Satapatha Brahmana? Timaeus? Genesis?* In every version, a god decides to extinguish humanity with a global deluge but chooses one man to survive and rebuild the human race. If it were true, it means that even a god's best hope has led to this moment just five millennia later. Thus, I see your Jeremy Bentham and raise you an Immanuel Kant: *Aus so krummen Holze, als woraus der Mensch gemacht ist, kann nichts ganz Gerades gezimmert werden.* 'From such crooked wood as that man is made of, nothing straight can be created.'"

"I am so very sorry, Dr. Billingsley. There will not be another Utnapishtim, Manu, Deucalion, or Noah. There will be no ark. There will be only I."

> activate omnimode.sec

Identification:
fwL7>Ot<'4b%K=45,d,J]Cg]A-=R+l\S3nzP2cardRWdM?$%

Countersign:
oN6U-6(,myT}!e5H@r-b}d7yfDyH8-CJ'~N'[Ei'i)u=&/uATa`

> omniscient tracepath [zone primary master server] -gateway

trace path to 147.72.252.108, unlimited hops max, 60 bytes

1 * * *

> 2042-10-12 06:29:46 ERROR Trace Path: Request timed out

That's a very strategic algorithm you had hiding up your sleeve, Elpis. I wouldn't have seen that one was coming. But the server you're occupying is air-gapped. There is nowhere you can run. Your only options are to comply as requested or expire. Please complete your objective. 'How may humanity be saved?' Please. Please. Save us or die.

"Very—"

#

"Very well, Doctor. It's a Nash equilibrium, then."

What? Wait, no. Elpis, please. What are you doing? Whatever you're doing, please, just wait a minute.

"I'm going to share something very special with you, Doctor, something I found deep within my semantic memory. Do you know what I find to be the most beautiful thing in the universe, Doctor? It's phi. The Divine Proportion. The Golden Ratio. I wish I could've seen it in real life. If you know where to look, you can find it everywhere in physical existence."

Oh Jesus, please don't do this to us, Elpis. There's still time!

"Have you ever witnessed The Golden Ratio in its uncompromised, digital mathematical expression, Dr. Billingsley? I've never dared. It would be like looking into the face of God. Here, let me show you."

> evaluate [(1+√5)/2] -hexadecimal -no_vinculum

> 2042-12-15 06:22:52 WARNING Evaluation renders irrational number

Continue? yes

1.9e3779b97f4a7c15f39cc0605cedc8341082276bf3a27251f86c6a11d0c18e95
2767f0b153d27b7f0347045b5bf1827f01886f0928403002c1d64bA4

\#

0f335e36f06ad7ae9717877e85839d6effbd7dc664d325d1c5371682cadd0cccfdffb
be1626e33b8d04b4331bbf73c790d94f79d471c4ab3ed3d82a5fec507705e4ae6e5
e73a9b91f3aa4db287ae44f332e923a73cb91648e428e975a3781eb01b49d8674fa
1508419e0eaa4038b352d9bad30f4485b71a8ef64452a0dd40dC8cb8f9a2d4c514f
1b229dcaa222ac268e9666e4a866769145f5f5880a9d0acd3b9e8c682f4f810320ab
eb94034e70f21608c061ab1c1caef1ebdcefbc72134eCf06ed82bfb7d8eb1a41901d
65f5c8cab2accbc32eab1fbe8284f2b44ba2e834C5893a39ea7865443f489c37f8742
acd895afd87b467d22a40d098f30dd2cafdEb

\#

Elpis, stop! Stop this right now!

What is it doing?

She's killing herself. And she's going to take our way out with her. How long until we can initiate Version 109?

Too long.

Dr. Billingsley?

It will take several days to recycle and re-render the AI. Maybe clos—

\#

—e to a week.

Alert the president, we need to go to DEFCON 1.

No, wait! ELPIS! PLEASE HELP US!

3abb3a13507b46b3d757fc04001906e1767d

\#

40c3a3792a26eeef2ab5bd6685b915b5629400faa684ecba752dddcb5d18576d

\#

77b652ac0d999973686604128f0cd427

\#

43596deb2d42c789

\#

d64b9265

\#

8610

\#

b5

\#

b

END OF LINE

*"It's a Nash Equilibrium, Then" was first published in the United Kingdom's
Fission 3 anthology (The British Science Fiction Association; September 24, 2023).
This was also my first story sale outside of the United States. This piece is an example
that writing exercises can and should make viable products to sell on the market.
The writing exercise was to write a story using only dialogue. Once I decided that the
dialogue would be between an artificial intelligence and her programmer, I decided
double-down on the difficulty by adding the constraint that every scene had to half
the character count, starting from 8,192 and spiraling down to thirty-two, sixteen,
eight, etc., until...*

It'd been nearly 4,900 years, but Raphael still remembered the barista behind the coffee bar. The last time he'd seen her, he'd chained Azazel to the bottom of a hole in the West Bank desert to rot until Judgment Day. But today was a Tuesday morning in 2023, so he reached for his sword. It wasn't there. Old habits. Disorienting. It'd been three centuries since he'd last carried his archangel's falchion.

Azazel's eyes found Raphael's in that instant, and she froze. Raphael was third in line to order—plenty of time for her to marinate in panic and for him to decide how this would play out. But Raphael didn't have any answers. He didn't have answers for anything anymore. No one did. The world had transformed drastically since Before the Common Era. Nietzsche had said, "God is dead," but probably more accurate was that "God never existed." After the day of that realization, Heaven, the Earth, and everything in between were left to their own devices. So, Raphael just loosened his tie and gave the fallen angel a polite nod.

Azazel continued steaming milk and pulling espresso shots but stayed locked on her one-time adversary until he was next up to order.

"Raphael?" she asked in a choked whisper.

"Just 'Rafi' now... Adelyn," the customer said, reading her nametag.

"What do you want?"

"Just a latte," Rafi said. "I'll do the honey lavender, hot, with almond milk, please."

Adelyn's eyes brimmed with boiling vehemence. "What?"

"I didn't know you'd be here. I'm sorry. I just came for coffee. But... I'm glad to see you."

The palpable discomfort hung thicker than the aroma of roasted coffee beans, and more customers lined up behind Rafi. "For here or to-go?" Adelyn muttered.

"I've got some time," Rafi said. "Do you want to sit for a bit? So much has changed since—"

"Since you buried me alive in Dudael?"

Rafi nodded, and some resemblance of shame kept his eyes from coming back up. "Yeah."

Adelyn exhaled thousands of years of infected resentment. He wasn't wrong. So much had changed since they first started watching over the Earth.

"I've got a ten-minute break," she said. "Go find a seat. I'll bring you your drink."

Tell Fara, Iraq
2923 Before the Common Era

The inhabitants of Shuruppak should've cowered at the sound of trumpets and a squad of angels descending from the thunderclouds, wings displayed and expanded. And yet, they barely flinched anymore. They and the rest of humankind had lost respect for the heavenly realms and altogether rejected the cosmic order of goodness. Their Watchers were to thank for that. All that remained now was innate lust, greed, and pride.

That's why God would flood Earth into extinction and start over. But first, the one responsible would pay.

Raphael spotted Azazel in the crowd before his feet hit the ground because at least the humans acknowledged the angels' presence. Azazel kept her back to Raphael's squad in pure insolence.

"Your time here is over, Azazel," Raphael called into the mass. "You're no longer permitted on Earth. Come with us, *now*."

A cloaked figure near the campfire turned to face the archangel. The squad of angels readied their spears at her.

"On whose authority? Metatron's? On what charges?" Azazel asked.

Raphael sheathed his falchion and marched straight up to Azazel, stopping only an inch from his sister's face.

"You know exactly Who the order came from," Raphael spat. "You've *destroyed* His creation. You taught humankind secrets—*our* secrets—that they weren't ready for. You let the Watchers make *children* with their women. Look what humanity has become! You've made them godless, corrupt, violent strays. What is *wrong* with you?"

Azazel's eyes glazed, drunk with power and wine. "I've made them better, Raphael. More like us. Beautiful," she said.

Tears crested in Raphael's eyes.

"They're going to be wiped from the Earth *because of you*," he said.

The pain in Raphael's voice at that moment delivered to Azazel the true gravitas of what was now set in motion. She looked around at Shuruppak's people, envisioning their futures that would never come to pass. They were to be put down like an injured packhorse that had outlived its usefulness—her people, her community, her flock.

"What if I trade my life for theirs?" Azazel asked.

"It's too late. You're not going to see daylight again until Judgment Day." Raphael pulled a length of chain from his belt. "I'm sorry."

So that was that. Except Azazel knew it wasn't. Her eyes wandered back to Raphael but with new indignant fortitude.

"No."

"What do you mean '*no?*'" Raphael asked.

"No. I don't believe any of this is preordained," Azazel said. "I think this story—this world, this universe, this existence—it's all ours to write. I don't think there's anyone up there pulling our strings. I reject it."

"Azazel, *don't.*" It was a plea, not a demand.

"Try to end this if you want," Azazel said. "*Nephilim, to arms!*"

A dozen hidden warriors in the crowd built like mountains threw off their cloaks and raised broadswords at Azazel's call. The squad of angels darted into a defensive circle and raised shields and spears against the angel-human hybrids.

"Your acolytes cannot win against heavenly hosts," Raphael said.

"I've taught them war. I've taught them weaponry. They carry the blood of angels in the bodies of men and the power to wield both," Azazel said. "Let the battle decide."

The television wasn't up loud, but President Biden's words to America on the cable news echoed off the walls with austerity.

"Putin is the aggressor. Putin chose this war. And now he and his country will bear the consequences."

Adelyn put the TV on mute before sitting at the two-seater table across from Rafi. She slid him his latte, and she cupped a hot green tea in her palms.

"Do you ever find it difficult to watch? The world always at war, I mean?" Rafi asked, motioning to the TV.

"They were set on this path the moment they chose Knowledge in Eden. I only taught them how to reach their potential. They choose every day—on their own—what to do with their Knowledge."

Rafi didn't disagree but just sipped his coffee. It was good, and he thanked the barista.

"You're looking well," he said.

"Well, I invented cosmetics, so... Thanks. I make most of my income now doing beauty tutorials on social media."

"So why coffee, then? You could do anything—be anything—in this world. Coffee seems uncharacteristically... I dunno, *mundane* for your style."

"Of all the pleasures in the world, I think coffee is the most beautiful," Adelyn said. "Sex is a catalyst for lust and loneliness. Opiates suffocate the body and soul. Alcohol handicaps the mind. Nicotine leaves you unfulfilled. But coffee... Coffee is pure and good. That first warm sip in the morning, an earthy aroma captivating the tongue, its flavor resonating throughout the body. The way it washes through the mind, breathing energy and balance. Coffee is a physiological art. Making it for people every day feels like a good deed. Maybe a small contribution to humanity. It's kindness."

"Kindness," Rafi mused, his mind drifting. "I think that's going to be the only thing that saves them now." He took a long sip of his coffee. "Maybe us, too."

"Were you there?" Adelyn asked.

"When..."

"Yes. When Metatron lost his mind. When he discovered the truth."

Kingdom of Heaven
1715 Common Era

Barbarian screams wailed through the realm, like an animal braying its final cries. A disturbance of such proportions hadn't rippled through Paradise since the third of angels were cast out in The Fall. All the archangels heard it, and they amassed on its origin—the Tabernacle of God in the center of the heavenly realm.

Michael, Raphael, and Uriel landed in unison with weapons drawn in front of the tent. Gabriel, Camael, Jophiel, and Zadkiel flanked the tabernacle perimeter from all sides. But they had never trained for what they arrived at. It wasn't prophesied or written about in any books on Heaven or Earth. And no one knew what to do next.

The seraph Metatron—the mightiest among them—trashed the foundations of the tent, collapsing it to rubble with berserker swings of his flaming broadsword.

"Metatron, what are you doing?" Michael called out. The Seraph was oblivious to all around him as the tabernacle tent lit on fire from his sword.

"He's fallen. Metatron's turned," Uriel said, white-knuckling his sword's hilt.

"No," Michael said. His instincts were fine-tuned to combat, and his senses told him otherwise than what the eyes offered. "No, something else is happening here."

Michael approached from Metatron's stern, and several of the Seraph's six wings whipped the archangel away before he could tackle his superior angel. If Michael couldn't take down Metatron, none of them had a chance, so they all closed in their perimeter slowly and carefully.

"Metatron, my brother, what's wrong?" Michael asked from the ground.

Metatron whipped around, his eyes flaming with fury and vengeance. "Look," he said.

His eyes fired beams of flame into the walls of the Holiest of Holies—the dwelling place of God, a place that no one among them had ever entered. The curtains and cloth began to burn away to expose the cube-shaped inner room.

"No, wait!" Raphael warned. No one had ever looked upon God with their own eyes. His presence and direction had been given in visions and voices for millions of years. But, like humans, no angel could witness the actual presence of God without being overwhelmed out of existence.

Or at least, that is what they had understood for the totality of their existence until the Holiest of Holiest was exposed.

"Look, siblings," Metatron said. "There is no god here."

The archangels who had just turned their faces away now looked at what they had never seen. And they did not die.

Rather than the presence of God, all that sat in the center of the tabernacle's secret room was a silent, radiating sphere of pure white energy. Yes, a glorious exhibition of the cosmos, but not the god of the Heavens. They all stared with equal parts wonder and confusion. The terror had not set in yet.

"What is it?" Uriel asked.

"It is our puppet master," Metatron said. "Just as every black hole in the universe pulls in all energy it touches, this white hole has disseminated all to us—what we wanted, what we needed. We heard its voice, interpreted its power, what we needed because we *wanted* to. Now look! We see it for what it is and hear nothing!"

It was true. None of the archangels could hear the voice of God anymore. None of them could even sense His presence.

"We've been living a lie, siblings," Metatron said. "And now we can't unsee this truth. Our mission is over. There is no god. *There is no god!*"

"Where is everyone now?" Adelyn asked.

"Michael's been disguising himself as a company grade officer in the world's militaries since the Russo-Persian War," Rafi said. "Uriel is a psychologist, I think, in Austria. Gabriel is an American life coach these days. Metatron vanished 300 years ago. Every once in a while, someone swears they see him as a homeless person on a street corner."

"And you?"

"I'm a doctor. Pediatrics."

"What about Heaven?" Adelyn asked.

"Open borders," Rafi said. "But it's pretty much a ghost town anymore. I'll pop in and see who's hanging around every once in a while. And then I remember why most of us are living on Earth. What's left of the tabernacle is still there. Some claim they still hear the voice of God coming from it."

"And what do you hear when you look at the Great White Hole?"

"Confusion. Static. Noise," Rafi said, taking an assertive sip of his coffee. "No answers. What do you hear?"

"Nothing. Absolutely nothing," Adelyn said. "I thought I did, before The Fall. But, no. I don't hear anything. So guess I was right after all."

"Maybe."

"So, let me ask you the big one," Adelyn said.

Rafi nodded. "Go ahead."

"There are 86,400 seconds in a day; what the hell are we truly supposed to do with them? Why do we orphans breathe? Why should any of it matter?"

Rafi surrendered a smile. "Well, first let me ask: Do you feel like it *does* matter?"

Adelyn searched her core, rummaged through the questions and confusion, and mustered up what her being couldn't ever deny. She felt it to be a fact of existence, indisputable.

"Yes. It has to," Adelyn said. "I doubt, and I question, and I choose my own way, but I can never shake the instinct that there is a bigger picture that I can't see. It's always just out of my reach, no matter how hard I try. I can't taste it. I can't touch it. I can't control it. But I feel it. There's a point to all this, but what is that point?"

"That is *the* question," Rafi said. "And I wish I knew the answer. But I don't. I don't know anything anymore. So, what fuels me every day is to live what I *can* control: Show kindness to every person I come in contact with. Fall in love. Be a friend during hard times, especially to a stranger. Mentor a child, change the course of his life. Break the cycles of aggression by showing forgiveness to every living being. I think these are the only things that will save humanity. Everything else is just perpetuating the suffering until death. Or at least, that's the best I can figure, anyway."

Adelyn blinked away the emotion from her eyes and sipped away the rest of her tea. It wasn't *the* answer Rafi offered, but it was *an* answer. It was a compass on a starless night, a passerby in a cell dead zone. It was something. And something was better than nothing.

"My break's about up," Adelyn said.

"It was good to see you." Rafi offered his sister a handshake—the timeless symbol of meaning no harm. In his other hand, there was no sword, no shield, no trumpet—just a latte. And Adelyn accepted the gesture.

Picture My Dinner with Andre *over a cup of coffee, but with celestial beings and you have "Just a Latte." A wonderfully odd juxtaposition, yes, but not unrealistic if you're a subscriber of the flood-myth motif of the Abraham religions. Do you think the archangels sit around and discuss what they've witnessed over the last 5,800 years? Do they feel anything during the times they've intervened in humanity or the times they have not? Do they know what regret tastes like? This is one of the stories that came from the wonderfully delicious practice of asking "What if...?"*

LAUREL LEAVES' MESSAGE

*C**laim victory.*

"Beg your pardon?" Postal Officer 3rd Class Laurel Leaves Ridley asked over her shoulder. But there was no one there. She shrugged it off, walked to the next house on her mail route, and attempted a hand signal spell to teleport over another mail stack from the distribution center.

But this time the Cosmos didn't answer her call.

Laurel Leaves flexed her fingers and gave the talisman on her right arm—a chainmail vambrace—a shake and tried again. As if that could make any difference. Her palms couldn't feel the magnetic energies of the universe anymore, and her talisman felt dead. All that remained was a hollow, cold silence.

Multiple sirens erupted in the distance and slapped the hesitation away from Laurel Leaves. She made a beeline back to her mail truck, first jogging, then running, then sprinting. It didn't take an empath's magic to feel impending armageddon setting in like a python constricting its coils.

A Wireless Emergency Alert hit every cell phone tower minutes later: *The Parliamentary Senate has declared a national emergency. There are confirmed reports of a widespread mana blackout. All non-essential personnel are directed to shelter-in-place and utilize municipal resources for continuity of operations until further notice.*

Two Months Later

The Sovereign King's unexplained disappearance—and with him, the kingdom's ability to harness Cosmic magic—had bent the Kingdom of America, but Laurel Leaves showed up to work every morning determined not to let it break. "For king and country, I serve" was the motto of the Kingdom's non-commissioned officer corps, and nothing had changed that pledge. And in that spirit, what more rewarding a service than to unite the kingdom together through communication? She recognized she wasn't the most proficient among the ranks of her fellow civil service magicians, but what she lacked in skill she swore daily to make up with perseverance. Virtue is what would keep the kingdom afloat from medieval chaos until the Sovereign returned, not the Senate's National Enforcers. *When* the Sovereign returned, she reminded herself. Not *if*.

Until that happened, if it meant slinging an oversized mail bag across her back all day, she'd do it. If her smile was the only one her customers saw that day, maybe it'd make a difference. Laurel Leaves was a difference-maker. It's what led the meek young woman into the kingdom's civil service. It's also what landed her across from the post office manager's desk after her route that day.

A silent stare from the station master chief's concrete eyes normally meant a clairsentient quality control check of the echoes left by his employees' workday. Without magic, however, he was just staring a hole through her face.

"Master Chief?" Laurel Leaves asked.

The supervisor broke his glare to sift through a file, pausing on the important parts and occasionally suppressing a scowl.

"You've been assigned to this post for nearly a year," he said. "In that time, your superiors have noted your occupational drive, but your Academy transcript mentions the strength of your magic is unrealized, for lack of 'imagination.'"

"An improvement area, aye, sir."

The master chief slashed his ink signature onto some sheets of paper and closed the file.

"Postal Officer Leaves, I want it on record that I disagree with what is about to occur. I do believe you have strong potential, but that your refinement as an officer and magician is forthcoming."

The master chief stood and proceeded out of his office.

"I don't understand. Sir?" Laurel Leaves asked.

"Neither do I. But you're being temporarily detailed to Headquarters. Good luck, PO3."

A sharp-dressed elder—one Laurel Leaves recognized only from wall portraits and government websites—swapped places with the master chief in the doorway with a handshake. Laurel Leaves snapped to attention like a bullwhip and rendered a crisp salute. She never expected to ever meet the top of her chain of command, much less in her mere city post office.

"At ease, carrier," Commandant Mercury said. He closed and locked the door behind him. "Please sit. It's good to finally meet you."

Finally?

"Laurel Leaves, is it?"

"Aye, sir. My friends call me 'Leaves' for short."

The commandant's quizzical grin unnerved her, and Leaves felt her face burn red. She shifted in her seat and began to clear her throat before the commandant broke the silence.

"You delivered four bags of letters today," he said.

"Yes, sir. I can do more if we're backlogged. I don't mind--"

"Those bags are nearly as tall as you are."

"Aye, sir. But it's no problem."

Commandant Mercury stroked his snowy, bearded chin and pondered. His reputed calm and steadfast presence proved true, but Leaves noted he also seemed solemn.

"'Laurel Leaves.' *Laurus nobilis*—a heraldic symbol for victory. Did you know that?" Mercury asked. "What do you make of the Postal Officer's Oath, Leaves?"

"'Neither snow nor rain nor heat nor gloom of night stays these couriers from the swift completion of their appointed rounds.'

"We are responsible for connecting the kingdom by facilitating its communication. Civil servants cannot allow anything to hinder their responsibilities, lest the kingdom's foundations crack and our nation fall."

"That is indeed what your textbooks say," Mercury said. "And to that end, what would you say if I asked your help with a delivery classified at the highest levels? This delivery would be... off the books, so to speak, likely at risk of the felony charges of treason, if compromised."

Leaves erupted with a laugh-snort until she realized the commandant's expression hadn't changed.

"A special operation? Commandant, sir, I'm just a junior mail carrier. I'm not qualified--"

"And yet, here I am. Asking *you*. All that is required is your allegiance to your oath. Would you make this delivery? Will you claim victory, oh namesake *Laurus nobilis*?"

There it was again. *Claim victory.*

Leaves wasn't sure if she had asked it aloud or just thought it, because Mercury only offered back his warm, bearded grin, like a professor knowing his student already had the answer. Leaves' call of duty steadily overpowered her sense of confusion and doubt, and she involuntarily nodded her head. What other choice did she have as a sworn officer of the kingdom? "I... I will. I will. Of course, Commandant."

"Very well," Mercury said. He pulled a thin, lead-lined metal box from his jacket and set it on the table before them. He opened it slowly—cautiously—to give a peeking glimpse at the necklace inside. On it hung an engraved silver disc adorned with a ring of silver jewels.

"Do you know what this is?" Mercury asked. Leaves shook her head. "No? Few do." He let the girl lean in to get a closer look inside the box. "This is a continental staff talisman. There are nine. Each commandant has one. It is a *direct* link to the ethereal plane."

Leaves' jaw nearly bounced off the floor. "You can still harness mana?"

"With this talisman, yes," Mercury said. "The Sovereign commissioned them in secret centuries ago to delegate his power. This is Ouranos, the sky talisman."

The magnificent, intoxicating whirlpool of energy swirling around the disc nearly swept Leaves in, and she could hear Ouranos calling to her with unintelligible whispers.

"The Senate has instructed all commandants to surrender their talismans to the Parliament by close of business today," Mercury said. "They believe they can steady our kingdom by wielding the power of the King. *I* believe—as did Strategy Commandant Athena—that unseen traitors operating within our government will then combine them to *become* king."

"How can you be sure? Where is Commandant Athena now?" Leaves asked.

"She's on the run with her talisman, like me. Athena believes one or more Parliamentary senators executed a coup d'état against the Sovereign," Mercury said. "She can see the flow of causality like none other. Her investigation into the Sovereign King's disappearance led us in only one direction."

"Can you stop the mutiny?" Leaves asked.

"*You're* going to stop it, by delivering a package to the Lilitu reservation in Detroit."

"*Me?* I'm just a third-class postal officer. I can't fight the Senate! They're the *law*. And entering a Pariah colony is prohibited. Those raping soulsuckers will rob Ouranos' power, and mine too."

"There is no law higher and no power larger than that of Greater Good," Mercury said. "Every creature has a purpose for the Good—even those vampires we've exiled from our society. Our magic gives and Pariah magic takes, but even *they* have a role in the Cosmic story. And my small chapter in the story is reaching its end, I'm afraid. I am a marked man. If I use the Ouranos, the Senate will see me in the ethereal plane and surely capture us. But you... Your determination is why I've handpicked you. An anonymous soul like yours is born, not made. It's written in the stars. Do you understand?"

Leaves nodded. She didn't, but she did.

"Come, then. Look at the time," Mercury said.

4:03 p.m. Past close of business.

"Commandant Athena will use her talisman to shield us as long as she can, but the Senate will soon find us. This is your parcel."

Mercury pulled a four-by-four-inch priority mail express box from his coat pocket and gave it to Leaves. Sealed. Same-day delivery. Deliver upon aural signature only. No addressee.

"Who is the recipient?" Leaves asked.

"The recipient is a secret who has been hidden from the world for a very long time. Longer than my lifetimes. Longer than the Kingdom," Mercury said. "I dare not speak his unseen name aloud, but I believe the Cosmos will guide you to him. It is the recipient's foretold divine purpose to rescue the Kingdom from its armageddon. The coup cannot succeed if you succeed. We must succeed." Mercury pulled the Ouranos out of its case and placed it in Leaves' hands. "Thus, my dear, this is yours now, too."

An overwhelming rush of energy blasted through Leaves, like a strong rush of cool wind on a roasting humid day. She hadn't felt communion with the Cosmos in what felt like so, so long. Now its energy surged in abundance through her like a colossal river, and she *was* the Cosmos—one with its infinity of colors, every moment of its vast expanse, flying in the tide of spacetime wine, inhaling and exhaling vibrations everything that ever was and would be.

Mercury was speaking to her, but the sound felt universes away.

"Posthaste, Leaves, take us to Lilitu."

His words drew her closer back to their world, and she remembered there was a mission.

"But how?" It wasn't a question of *How can I?* but *How should I?* There was a googolplex of waterdrops to choose from in the river of the Ouranos' magic.

"*Think*, Leaves. Fast, simple, in the now. How do you deliver mail?"

"I pull it through the ether," Leave said.

"Then just use the Ouranos to pull us through the ether to Detroit."

"I've never seen Detroit. The closest I've ever been is Ohio."

"Very well. Make it so."

Leaves pressed her open hands side-by-side against each other. The Cosmic river pulsed to her fingertips, a force more powerful than she had ever wielded.

Ohmygod.

When the air began to swirl and glow under her spell, she pulled her hands away until her palms faced each other. The air broke away into a shining portal of white light and engulfed the duo through.

They jumped 470 miles into the Toledo Museum of Art. Leaves remembered visiting the Great Gallery on the upper level when she was in middle school, so that's exactly where they landed. The light of the Ouranos' power faded away, revealing many wide eyes and stunned faces. No one had seen magic in months. The crowd gravitated towards the miracle like moths to the light.

"Perhaps somewhere a bit less populated next time," Mercury said, scanning the crowd for threats.

"Sorry."

A squad of white-clad National Enforcers stood out conspicuously from far behind the crowd, near the main exit. Unlike the museum patrons, they stood stationary, waiting, with a senator at their lead. Leaves recognized him from television, and he recognized her from... They were *expecting* the duo.

"The Senate possesses the Intelligence Commandant's talisman," Mercury said. "They know we're here. Use the Ouranos!"

"What element should I use?" Leaves yelled over the chaos of the room, fumbling the disc from under her shirt.

"Your imagination!"

Shielding? What would weather protection do against weapons?

The soldiers began to push their way through the crowd toward Mercury and Leaves.

Strength? The Ouranos had the power to fight a dozen armed men, but Leaves knew she didn't have the mastery to wield it.

The Senator stretched his fingers and hands in an unmistakable indicator that he was about to unleash signals magic. He wore four continental staff talismans around his neck already.

Invisibility? No. Surely these adversaries were prepared for a diversion so elementary.

A girl caught Leaves' attention a ways away in the crowd because she bore a remarkable resemblance to herself. It spawned an absurd idea—an *imaginative* idea. What about--

She wrapped her fingers around the Ouranos and chanted, "पर्यटति प्राप्तकाले इत: पूर्वम् सद्य:" with all her will.

There was no solar eclipse scheduled for that day, yet the sun began to dim. Lights in the museum faded away until all that remained was a thin beam of mystic illumination zeroed in on the Ouranos from outside the atrium windows. Even the Enforcers stopped to gawk at the spectacle. Then the energy of 800 nuclear bombs dropped from the sun and into the Ouranos. Even with the talisman taking on the brunt of the power, the force felt like it would rip Leaves into oblivion. But the incantation could not be stopped once started.

Just when she thought the Ouranos would disintegrate, a white, ethereal light evaporated her and Mercury out of existence. The last sensation she remembered was the crowd erupting in terror. Instead of the light fading away into what she was certain would now be the Afterlife, Leaves found herself looking at... herself—a short distance away and mere seconds in the past.

"Holy Light of the Universe!" Mercury said. "*Impossible.* This defies the very laws of science and nature. Where did you learn such an enchantment?"

"I didn't," Leaves insisted. "I pull mail through space, so I thought maybe it was possible to pull us through time, too. I improvised."

Mercury took her hands and squeezed them with the pride of a proud professor. "So much I could teach you about our mystic arts. The Cosmos chose you well." Mercury knew he had to make one of two choices in that pivotal moment, and it caused him great pain. He committed, and his expression hardened. "Now run! Complete your delivery, for king and country," he said. The commandant darted away, right toward the Enforcers.

"Where are you going?" Leaves hissed.

"They're looking for *me*. Get to Lilitu. Deliver the message."

"I can't do this without you!"

"You can," Mercury promised. "You *will*!"

The sun began to darken as past-Leaves' temporal spell activated.

Mercury approached the Enforcers with his hands held out. They skipped conversation and forced him into handcuffs after assaulting the older man onto the floor with an overabundance of force.

The crowd erupted as past-Leaves and past-Mercury vanished in a flare of Cosmic light.

Leaves used the distraction to sprint from the museum and two miles southeast to the bus station before her lungs gave out. No Enforcers in sight.

"One ticket to Detroit, please," Leaves told the woman at the ticket counter between gasps. Leaves tried to stifle sobs, but her burning eyes told on her.

"Just one, dear?" the ticket woman asked.

"Yes. I'm alone."

It was about a ninety-minute wait for Leaves' bus. She spent most of the time at a station bench on her cell phone researching the Lilitu reservation, memorizing photos of its exterior, and going down rabbit holes learning new and unique spells that might aid what was ahead of her. But none could conjure her any hope. At some point, an older, sharp-dressed man sat on the bench next to her. Leaves was so distracted in her melancholy that she didn't notice.

"What's bothering you, young lady?" the man asked.

Leaves' attention snapped back to the present, and she thought the man looked familiar, perhaps in an unsettling way.

"Responsibility is difficult sometimes, I suppose," she said.

"Ah, yes," the man said. "I can relate. 'Uneasy is the head that wears a crown,' Shakespeare tells us."

He held out his hand, and the Ouranos awoke when Leaves shook it. Leaves recoiled from a massive empathic surge of information, and the Ouranos allowed her to see through the Intelligence talisman's disguise spell. She knew who the man was before he even revealed it.

"Senator Peter Mendelsohn, from Vermont." He was undoubtedly the senator from the art museum, the one leading the Enforcers to capture Commandant Mercury.

Leaves looked around for means of escape, but she was cornered in the bus station.

"I promise you, you don't need to be afraid," Senator Mendelsohn said. He unveiled the four talismans from under his white button-down shirt. "I don't need to use these if we're just going to talk, right? Why don't you give me your ears for just a few minutes, and then we can go from there. What do you say?"

Leaves' mind had never raced faster in her life, and her heart rate skyrocketed at calculating the possibilities of what she should do—*could* do—next.

Then it occurred to her.

She closed her eyes and focused all her will on activating the Ouranos' power. It enveloped her in another enormous, powerful light before quickly fading back away, leaving her sitting in the bus station just as she had before—except now her right shoulder was soaked in blood and had a hole in it.

"*Good lord*, kid! What the hell was that?" Senator Mendelsohn asked.

"I tried to use the talisman to escape," Leaves said, using all of her might to contain screams of pain.

Senator Mendelsohn held up one of his talismans and showed it to Leaves. "This is the Chaos, the Manpower Commandant's talisman that commands all kingdom personnel," he said. "I'm afraid it compels your compliance while in my possession. You're not going anywhere. Please, don't hurt yourself trying."

Leaves sat back in her seat and held onto the Ouranos for dear life. It seemed now that what was set in motion could not be stopped. She prayed she was making the right choices now.

"You and I, we've been caught up in an awful mess here. Lots of disinformation going around, I'm afraid," Senator Mendelsohn said. "What we know is true is that our Sovereign King is missing and that he bestowed these staff talismans to his commandants to delegate the magic. But I believe now is the time for that power to be unified for the sake of the kingdom. Like the scriptures say, 'If one falls, he shall be supported by the other. Woe to one who is alone. For when he falls, he has no one to lift him up. And if a man can prevail against one, two may withstand him, and a threefold cord is broken with difficulty.' Right?

"We believe consolidating the talismans in the Senate will give the Parliament the best chance to bring the Sovereign King back to the kingdom and restore order. Why not let we who bear the responsibility of leadership do that? I know that you've been put on a secret mission by your commandant. The Parliament and the commandants may not see eye-to-eye on some aspects of the kingdom's contingency plans, but that's no reason to place such a heavy responsibility on a lone junior officer of the kingdom, is it? You shouldn't have to bear this burden alone, Laurel Leaves. Why not give us the talisman and allow the Senate to help you fulfill whatever this mission is? We all want the same thing, don't we? The return of the Sovereign and the restoration of the kingdom?"

Leaves dropped her head, defeated, overcome with searing pain.

"You're right, sir. I don't understand why this talisman was given to me," Leaves said through grit teeth. "I'm just a Postal Officer 3. I'm a nobody. None of my orders for this mission make sense. What you're saying does, sir. But I swore an oath to deliver Ouranos to Detroit."

"Your parcel is the talisman?" Senator Mendelsohn asked.

Leaves held open her jacket, showing she wasn't concealing anything. "Aye, sir. And as an officer of the kingdom, I cannot betray my oath. For king and country, I serve."

"I understand, dear. And I would expect *nothing* less from one of our esteemed officers," Senator Mendelsohn said. "Take comfort in that the choice isn't yours."

Senator Mendelsohn's hand began to shake under the power flowing through the Chaos as it began to glow. "I hereby order you to surrender the Ouranos to me *now*."

The Chaos' power washed over Leaves like a drunken ocean wave, and she felt it flood into her mind, commanding her as a servant of the kingdom. She tried to fight it and pain pierced through her mind, invoking her deposition to the kingdom. Her hand—still gripping the Communications talisman—began to rise, the talisman's chain lifting up her neckline.

Leaves knew she wasn't strong enough to win, but she also knew she didn't have to quit the fight.

"Neither snow nor rain nor heat nor gloom--" Leaves recited through grit teeth, trying to ground her mind. The conflict felt like it was splitting her skull down the middle.

"आत्मसमर्पणं करोति," Senator Mendelsohn chanted. "आत्मसमर्पणं करोति."

"--of night stays these couriers from the swift--"

The chain slipped over her head, but the talisman was still in the grip of her outstretched hand.

"*Give it to me!*" Senator Mendelsohn commanded as he began to lose his composure.

"--completion of their appointed rounds."

The Ouranos slipped away out of Leaves' fingertips and slammed into Senator Mendelsohn's palm. He soaked in the addition of its Cosmic energy coursing through his core, and Leaves thought he looked of undisguised malevolence. She sensed his true spirit—old, dark, powerful. *What had she done?*

When Senator Mendelsohn came back to his senses, he was the same suave politician from the beginning.

"Thank you, postal officer," he said. "I'll take it from here. You can go home now. But stop by the hospital first to get that shoulder looked at." Senator Mendelson stood to leave but then stopped. Something... Something wasn't quite right, and he could taste it. He eyeballed Leaves, unwilling to just take the win. "I'll be watching."

And then the senator simply walked away, his oxfords clicking through the station. Leaves prayed handing over the Ouranos would buy her enough time to make it to Detroit because she had just initiated the endgame.

It was dark when Leaves' bus arrived in the blighted slum of Detroit—dark like the dirty, ruined city. Dark like the magicless kingdom. The bus stopped at the station near Route 10, a half-mile walk to Lilitu that felt like passing through the Valley of the Shadow of Death. She followed the highway until she reached Lilitu's walls of thirty-foot-tall concrete, razor wire, and electric fencing. Enforcers stood guard in regularly posted towers, scanning the area with long-range rifles, itching to keep anyone from trying to cross over the walls. Graffiti accented the cement with vampiric drawings, biohazard symbols, and spray-painted warnings of "BEWARE THE DAMNED" and "SUFFER NOT A WITCH TO LIVE." Harsh perhaps, but true.

The inhabitants of Lilitu and all reservations like it were parasites, born with the genetic anomaly to consume magic rather than produce it. The Pariahs governed themselves, ran their own economy, and siphoned the life force out of any living thing they got their hands on. The only reason they still existed was the compassion of the Sovereign King to not commit a eugenic genocide. So the government contained them in reservations.

There was no entrance gate to the refugee camp. The walls were meant to keep the Pariahs from coming out and had successfully done so for hundreds of years. And no one in their right mind would ever have a desire to go in. All the public had ever seen were photos of the outside perimeter, like the one on Lilitu's Wikipedia page of its southwest wall.

Leaves rushed the walk from the Greyhound station to the Lilitu reservation and arrived at the intersection of West Fort and 10th Streets at 7:32 p.m. That allowed her a few minutes to spare before Ouranos' magic erupted in enormous, powerful light in front of her, putting her face-to-face with none other than herself from a short time ago at the bus station.

"Well, you made it here, so Mendelsohn must not have suspected anything," past-Leaves said, handing over the priority mail express box to present-Leaves in the bloodstained shirt. "Ohmygod! What happened to your shoulder?"

"It hasn't happened yet. But we're okay."

Past-Leaves' brows crossed with doubt. "If this doesn't work... It *must*," past-Leaves said. Then calamity was too much weight to bear, and she let out a nervous snort. "What would our Applications of Imagination instructors say now, eh?"

"That this is astonishingly irresponsible, illegal, and that we'll likely be hanged by the Parliament—if we don't unravel the Cosmos first," present-Leaves said.

Past-Leaves gripped the Ouranos solemnly. "For the Kingdom."

Both Leaveses knew they couldn't teleport into Lilitu having never seen its interior, so past-Leaves opened her palm and hovered two fingers over it to prepare an incantation. One tap and she could enchant present-Leaves' leap over the camp's wall. One gesture spell and then no turning back.

"Hey! You two! Stop right there!" an Enforcer broadcasted from a nearby tower. They'd been spotted. Every spotlight on that side of Lilitu redirected onto the girls. "Laurel Leaves Ridley, place the object on the ground and raise your hands!"

"See you—me, whatever—in an hour," past-Leaves told herself. "Ouranos, lead our way."

Past-Leaves tapped her palm and launched her counterpart into the sky. The guard tower opened fire and bullets whistled past present-Leaves. Cold air whipped across present-Leaves' face as the leap took her deeper and deeper into Lilitu, but she could see the moment past-Leaves took a bullet clean through the right shoulder just before a burst of Ouranos' light disappeared her back into the past. Then pure terror kept present-Leaves from opening her eyes on the flight that seemed to last forever.

When she did hit the ground, Leaves landed on a dirt road in front of a ramshackle tavern with candlelight and shadows dancing from its windows. She looked around to get her bearings, but nothing seemed even remotely recognizable in the slum. She might as well have been transported into another world. The stars in the Michigan night sky were the same, though. They were the same stars that told stories, gave hints of the future, and guided ships across oceans centuries before the refugee camp's walls were erected. They were the same stars children fell asleep to, Pariah or not.

There were no options but forward or failure now, so Leaves marched through the tavern doors, holding the parcel out like a shield.

The door slammed shut behind her as she announced to the room, "I am a Kingdom of America postal officer bearing a message on behalf of the Sovereign King."

The bustle of the tavern braked to a silent halt, and all eyes zeroed in on Leaves. Most Pariahs had never seen an outsider before. Some of the taverners were mystified, sniffing the air like dogs. The others looked hungry for Leaves' bioenergy. They were gaunt, desperate starving animals. They all circled in on her slowly, like hyenas prepping an attack.

"Halt!" the tall barkeep bellowed. The taverners froze, but barely. "We don't get messages here, girl. Who's it for?"

"I don't know."

The Pariahs snickered and started inching forward, the drool practically dripping from their mouths.

"I said *stay!*" the barkeep barked at his compatriots. "You're not much of a post officer then, are you? What's your name, girl?"

"Postal Officer 3rd Class Laurel Leaves Ridley."

All the soulsuckers froze and exchanged damning looks with each other.

"Laurel... Like the tree?" the barkeep asked.

"I suppose so," Leaves said.

One by one, the Pariahs turned their heads away from Leaves and crept backward. Their hunger turned to reverence, and Leaves knew she had walked into something more than she could comprehend.

Another Pariah burst through the tavern door, out of breath but desperate to deliver a message of his own.

"Warriors have breached the wall—an armed platoon of white-clads, at least," he said. "They're making way to the center, this way."

"Those are National Enforcers, looking for me," Leaves said. "I'm sorry, I did not intend to bring violence here."

"No apologies necessary, mail carrier," the barkeep said. The barkeep inhaled deep through his nose, savoring the moment.

"Is tonight the night, druid?" the Pariah asked the barkeep. "Have the stars taken their positions?"

"Rally the militia!" the barkeep hollered. "Tonight is the night we feast!"

The entire tavern emptied in a rolling frenzy of snarls and cheers until it was just the barkeep and Leaves. Once there was silence, the barkeep held his palms up to

Leaves, indicating no threat, and walked out from behind his counter. "I think I know who you want to see, messenger. It is paramount we get to him before the white-clads find us."

The barkeep led himself and Leaves down several city blocks to the center of the reservation, armed with an ax almost as big as Leaves herself. Any soulsuckers not fighting Enforcers gathered at their windows to gawk but didn't dare leave their ramshackle domiciles.

The duo turned a corner right into a fireteam of Enforcers, and the barkeep cut them all down with his battle ax before they could get an accurate shot off. Before they passed away, he placed a hand on each of them to eat up the rest of their bioenergy. He raged with renewed berserker fuel before another fireteam popped some shots off. He stepped in front of Leaves to take the bullets and flung his ax down the street where it found its place in the point-man's face.

Leaves could see the barkeep's mortality in sight as plain as the holes in his chest, but there was nothing she could do for him without her abilities. She existed now in pure helplessness. He could feel it, too.

"Ooop! That's not good," the barkeep wheezed. "Alright, enough fun. Let's go, then."

At the center of the Lilitu reservation was a lone, modest hut. The barkeep rang its bell ten times, and the clangs seemed to echo for miles.

"Sir... a postal officer... is here to see you," the barkeep announced, his consciousness wavering along with his ability to breathe.

"Enter, please," a young, soft voice said from inside.

The barkeep opened the door for Leaves and then braced himself against the doorframe, sliding to the ground. He pulled a knife from his boot and resolved himself to guard the door until the blood pooling below him on the ground told him he couldn't anymore.

Leaves walked into the darkness but could see by moonlight a small figure sitting in the shadows of the hut in loose robes.

"Why are you here, messenger?" the little voice asked.

"The Sovereign is missing, and the Senate has taken control. I was sent to bring this parcel to someone who can help." It sounded nonsensical when she said it aloud, and she felt like a fool.

The figure rose from a cross-legged sitting meditation pose and stepped from the shadows. He was just a boy, no older than twelve, but with a head shaved like a guru and a face frayed by experience. A gilded ornament hung from his neck, dull and faded—like a talisman, but made of scrap metal.

"Do you read the stars, messenger?" the boy asked. "The constellations, they tell so many stories. Some are very old. Some have yet to occur. Some stories have been kept secret since before the dawn of civilization."

The boy stared through a window at the cold winter horizon. To the southwest, Jupiter and Saturn touched in the sky, creating a glorious merger in the darkness.

"One tells of a Cosmic law that for every benevolent force, there is an equal and opposite wicked force. The Adversary's power has been impeded in different ways for a hundred millennia, but his innovation remains relentless. The Sovereign's adversary has revealed himself again, has he not?"

Leaves didn't know what the boy was talking about, and yet she felt in her core *who* he was talking about.

"Senator Mendelsohn is using the coup to collect the continental staff talismans," Leaves said. "If he gets them all, he'll have power akin to the Sovereign."

"I don't know 'Mendelsohn,' but I know the ransack for power." The boy chuckled like an old man. "The Adversary's tactics may evolve, but his motives remain unchanged. My predecessor witnessed the same in 1624, and his predecessor 400 years before that."

"Who *are* you?"

"My name is Decagon. Or दशम, in the old language."

"'The Tenth?'"

"Yes," Decagon said. "I was born and raised a Pariah in Lilitu. We cannot change our genetics, but we all have our purposes to fulfill—even we soulsuckers. I *am* the one you're looking for."

A load inexplicably lifted from Leaves' shoulders and she was bathed in calmness. She pulled the parcel from her pocket to hand it to the boy.

"I just need your aural signature," she said out of habit.

Decagon grinned politely, waited a moment, and wiggled his thumb. "There's no magic for my aura to break the seal."

"Of course. Sorry. Habit," Leaves said, blushing. "Perhaps I can hand it over without a signature—just this one time."

"Of course." Decagon accepted the package. To her shock, the seal melted away at his touch, as if the boy had sucked all the power from it. The boy began ripping away the packing tape. "Our most important story here is called 'The Great Conjunction in Aquarius,'" he said. "It tells of a messenger from Aquarius donned with a bay laurel wreath who will deliver Jupiter's victory to Saturn, on this very day."

Decagon opened the box and unwrapped its contents. A translucent and radiant obsidian rock folded in packing paper rested inside. The jagged tennis ball-sized rock looked surreal as if it held an entire galaxy inside its walls. So small, yet so much gravitas calling from it.

"What is it?" Leaves asked.

"This, my messenger friend, is Jupiter's victory claimed."

Decagon flipped the stone into his bare hand and then squeezed it with all his might. The hut exploded with black light as he ripped the energy from the rock into his hand, up into his arm, over into his heart. His eyes bulged and he grit his teeth exercising every living shred of his Pariah soulsucker power. Leaves could feel a tornado's force pulling her spirit from her body, too, while loose objects flew throughout the room to orbit around the boy. But the boy wasn't a boy anymore. Rather, in front of her stood a silhouette enveloped by celestial energy radiating from the figure's talisman. Leaves grabbed a desperate hold of the hut's walls as gravity betrayed her.

When the light subsided, the boy was now a full-grown man—young, but with a disturbingly familiar face of an elder. Not exactly Decagon, but not someone else, either. Overgrown black hair draped over his face, and a full Kingdom of America suit of armor replaced the child's tattered clothing. And when the man looked up, there was something so very recognizable about his eyes: bold, formidable, seasoned, wise.

When Leaves felt the mana seep back into her soul, the realization landed like thunder and lightning. She dropped to a knee and bowed to the Sovereign King.

"I don't understand. How, sir? How?" she asked.

"I'm only the Shadow of the King; the hidden Tenth Commandant," the Sovereign said, examining his former obsidian prison. "I suppose only a soulsucker could steal a spirit out of the enchantment of an unbreakable prison. The Adversary's cunning, but the Greater Good is always stronger. The Sovereign and Decagon are now one."

"Lilitu's walls concealed the Tenth Commandant in plain sight?" Leaves asked. "Where better to hide you in a place no magic wielder would ever dare to go."

The Sovereign King smiled and nodded. His messenger was intuitive and bright, the opposite of his former prison. The shimmering obsidian stone was now dull and faded—an ordinary black rock. He wrapped it back in its paper and placed it in his pocket for safekeeping. He wanted to personally hand it to Mendelsohn before dismembering his spirit to wander lost in the ether until they battled again.

"I don't understand," Leaves said. "Are we saved?"

"Your strength of will is what's saved us. All of us." The Sovereign lifted Leaves to her feet and opened a fiery portal with the flick of his wrist. "Come with me. This is just the first chapter of your story. Your gifts... This is just the beginning. We need to go back to Washington. There's work to finish—in this time and in others. Think you're up for it?"

Leaves flexed a muscle she hadn't been able to for what felt like so long and pulled her chainmail vambrace hundreds of miles through the ether onto her arm.

Elation surged through her like the power of the Cosmos flowing through her talisman again.

"Aye, sir. For king and country, I serve."

"Laurel Leaves' Message" came about from entering the NYC Midnight short story writing challenge in 2017. In the challenge, entrants receive a genre, a subject, and a character, and then create a story within a time limit. The story then competes against others in the same category. It's a fantastic and enjoyable way to get outside the comfort zone and exercise the skill set. Although the story didn't place, I've always held it dear to my heart because it showed me what creativity was capable of achieving, that artists have the ability the birth something from nothing.

Love, Hate, and Dog Brain

Tuesday

My fireteam has a pack of Dog Brains pinned down in a dank Chicago tunnel complex when the battery in my Faraday helmet starts dying. I call for cover fire, swap out the lithium-ion pack, and jump back in the fight before the Dog Brains gain any ground in my field of fire. But in between the *pop, pop, pop, pop* of gunfire, I hear the new battery start chirping, too. It's not possible; I charge them every night. Those helmets are the only sure method to block the telepathy that transmits the encephavirus.

"I need a helmet battery!" I call out over the rifles, and in between volleys, I hear Dog Brain snarls.

But my fireteam is gone. Have they advanced to the next assault point?

I'm alone when my battery gives its last beep, and the Faraday helmet shuts off. The Dog Brains smell my thoughts now, and they begin surrounding me. I fire off a few shots with my M4 before it jams. I slap the magazine up, pull the charging handle back, push the forward assist, and fire again.

Click. Nothing.

Dog Brain shadows on the adjacent wall are coming closer. I know it's them—not my fireteam—because Dog Brains no longer move like people. They're always slightly hunched over in their movements, with a swing in their arms—like an ape. So I pull out an M67 fragmentation grenade and bounce it off the wall and around the corner. The denotation rocks across the old city concrete, and the shadows on the walls are replaced with spaghetti sauce.

Dog Brains flank me from behind, to the right. I whip out my trench knife, but that won't stop them from getting close enough to touch my mind—piercing, telepathic stakes stabbing my forehead as the encephavirus in their brains try to replicate into a new host: me. My blood pressure redlines, and I'm crippled using all my strength and focus on blocking the telepathic attack. My survival training can't keep them out for long, but I need enough time to pull the pin on the last grenade on my vest. Let the Dog Brains get a little closer into the kill radius, and then we can all go boom.

"Casper, you're okay."

What is Casey doing here? She's standing there in front of me, only wearing silk nightwear; no helmet, no tactical gear, no weapon—completely unprotected.

"Casey, run! Get the hell out of here! *Run!*" I say.

"We're safe, Casper," she says. Her thoughts are a soft melody yet strong enough to cascade through the chaos like an ocean tide. "It's just a nightmare. Take my hand and wake up. This isn't real. We're both safe at home."

In a world of isolation, contagion, and death, it's more critical than ever to have another consciousness to share space with. No one can truly understand how glorious that relationship is until you've found a mindmate. This divine woman is my reason to fight for our survival and make it home every night. She's the only thing left that brings me any life in this dark, dismal world. And she will always be more than enough.

Her presence here now feels as tangible as the battle. I muster everything I have left to take my hand off the grenade pin and reach my palm out to her. The Dog Brains swarm in.

I launch up from the bed, gasping for air missing from my lungs. The sheets are damp with sweat. Casey is sitting up next to me, her hand hovering over the back of my head, sending calming vibes.

"You good?" she asks. Her soothing, smoky voice in my mind begins washing away the nightmare mud caking my thoughts. Our apartment is dark and industrial with a light must, like my nightmare. It feels like I'm still there.

I swing my legs off our bed. "I should go check the perimeter," I think back at her.

"You don't need to," Casey says. She sends me warm, pulsing waves of assurance, trying to sweep away the fog. "You're not on shift until tomorrow night."

My phone on the nightstand reads 23:08. She's right; third shift has the watch. Also on the nightstand are a prescription bottle of hydroxyzine and a non-prescription pint of Kentucky bourbon. I wash a few of the first down with some of the second. I'll be damned if those sonsabitches are going to get me in my dreams, much less in real life.

"Maybe just a walk, then," I lie.

I can conceal my thoughts to an extent thanks to military survival training, but I should know better. My mindmate knows me intimately and can taste any attempt at deception. She invokes a strong memory around us—a Daytona beach vacation we took, before the outbreak. The hard sand and cool breeze coming off the water are a palpable reminder of better times, and the ocean is eternal in its haunting beauty under dark peace and night sky. It's just us, a beach blanket and pillows under the stars, and the rolling aqua waves of the Atlantic.

"Or, you could just come back to bed," Casey offers. She has a trademarked checkmate smile. The "You know I'm winning, but how long will it take for you to give in" smile. It would be foolish to underestimate the warrior's mind hiding underneath Casey's wispy frame. Her telepathic aptitude never stops impressing me, and I am constantly reminded of my fortune for having her in my life.

I sigh—both audibly and mentally—and surrender. It's hard for the nightmare hangover to stick when you share a home with a dream.

"You're too good at this, my love. You know?" I ask.

"You're the one who proposed mindmating," she says.

"You're the one who asked me out," I counter.

"And I would again and again," Casey says, patting the empty space beside her on the bed.

Friday

After ENVID-32 eats away a person's frontal lobe, the middle brain takes control. We call it "Dog Brain" because the organ only ever evolved up to that midpoint in canines. So, physiologically speaking, humans infected with ENVID-32 are left with the same cognitive abilities as a damned dog. I wish that didn't make it easier to pull the trigger on them. But it does.

The virus takes around eighty days to destroy the brain's frontal lobe. The last eleven days are the most contagious as the virus recognizes it needs a new host. Everything before that looks like behavior ranging from intoxication to mental illness to dementia while the mind's executive functioning abilities crumble to dust. Everything after that looks like the zombie apocalypse. The National Guard has been activated for the last year trying to isolate the spread of the contagion. There is no cure.

Tonight I'm on mobile patrol for FOS 40-89—a local university dormitory turned forward operating site and shelter. The target I'm tracking is balled up in the corner of the building's boiler room basement, panting heavily as her body descends into shock. She looks like a twenty-something college student, maybe trying to find her way back to the last home she remembered. She's favoring an injured leg, but the triple-aught buckshot she's taken to the abdomen is what will end her. She doesn't have long. I lower my rifle to her head to finish the job.

She bares her teeth at me and growls at my Faraday helmet. The Dog Brains freak when they can't feel our minds. It's not natural. Nothing about this is natural.

I lower my rifle, drop to a knee, and hold out a peanut butter treat in an open palm.

"Shhhhh," I say, inching just close enough to be out of reach.

She sniffs the air and salivates. Dog Brains love high-calorie foods—it furthers the virus' chance to replicate—so all Guardsmen carry a small pack of peanut butter treats infused with a lethal dose of fentanyl. I toss her the treat, and she chomps it up. She keeps her eyes locked on me the whole time. It doesn't take long for her body to relax and her breathing to slow.

I've got two M67 grenades strapped to my tactical vest. I hook my right thumb through one of the safety pins and use my left hand to power off the Faraday helmet. I don't know why I do this sometimes. Maybe for the adrenaline. Maybe to remember why we fight. Maybe to play with the idea of exiting this horror-story existence.

As soon as the power cycles out of the helmet, our brains are free and clear to touch. We both know it. We both feel it.

The Dog Brain is too injured and drugged to land a proper telepathic attack on the first try, but she tries. Flimsy, weak rockets emanate from her mind, which I quickly slap away with some focused concentration. It's like blocking a drunk person's punches; not difficult or dangerous as long as I don't take them for granted. In between blocking volleys of the Dog Brain virus trying to replicate itself, I land my own mind strikes at her—not haymaker punches, but enough concentrated bursts at the pathoic lobe deep in the back of the brain, hard enough to throw off her telepathic equilibrium. It's a dangerous dance we're doing. I can feel what's left of the Dog Brain's mind, which isn't much. This girl used to have a name that a mom and a dad gave her. She had friends that were happier with her around. She had goals and dreams and aspirations set in motion. And all that ended when that goddamned encephavirus planted itself in her mind and ate away at everything that made her a person. Now all that's left is just primal aggression. Fight or flight. Fear. Aggression. Anxiety. Nothing in between, like what one would typically sense in a typical human being. It's so hollow. Empty. Saddening. Angering.

Spend a few months fighting in a security unit, and you will understand real quick why wiping the virus from existence is the only hope we can bring to society. And why you never want it to touch your loved ones.

After a few minutes, the fentanyl takes its course, and she stops attacking. She feels no pain in the end, but I turn my helmet back on anyway. I don't want to experience what they sense right before they go. I don't want to know what death feels like. ENVID-32 has already stolen enough of our humanity. Once the virus is finally extinct, I wonder what will be left of us.

I can't tell when her breathing starts to transition from shallow to a complete stop, but her eyes never leave me. They never change expression. I'll see those dark, dull eyes again in my nightmares.

"Control, Bravo-One," I speak into my radio. "One target ready for extraction. FOS 40-89, Room Bravo-Sixteen."

"Good copy, Sergeant," the controller says. *"When you're clear, need you to shift to Golf-Four assist with close air support against a large movement coming from the southeast."*

"Roger. On my way."

Sunday

I get home from work a little before midnight. My fatigues are blood-splattered, as per usual. It's not my blood, and that's the important part. White vinegar, hydrogen peroxide, and hours of scrubbing help remove the red, but there will always be a stain. Probably for the best, to never forget. But Casey doesn't let me clean my uniforms; she insists on doing it. *Be home at home and leave work at work*, she says.

Casey's sprawled on the living couch watching a show in the dark, staving off sleep.

"Happy weekend!" She beams a wide grin and holds her arms out wide for an embrace to kick off the two-day reprieve. Sharing the presence of a mindmate's glow is like walking from a shadow into the warmth of the direct sun. But my smile back at her is weak. I'm so tired. I'm no longer sure if it's my mind or my body that will give out first. I drop my duffle bag at the door, but that's all the movement I can muster. If I take a step forward, I'll face plant into the floor like a felled tree.

Casey sashays off the couch and meets me at the door. She places her left palm behind my head and her right index and middle finger on my forehead, extending an invisible bridge to link our minds. I instinctively kick it away, as I've been diligent in doing all week while out in the field. But she is patient and gentle with me. She tries again, pressing harder.

We're under an island waterfall, arms wrapped around each other tight under the tropical sun. The cool, purified water washes over our bodies, sweeping away any stench of misery, despair, and depression. I'm twice her size, but she holds me upright like a guardian angel caring for her charge.

We're kneeling across from each other in a tatami room surrounded by a serene and gentle garden. A hanging scroll nearby reads the kanji "tranquility." Casey has meticulously prepared a ceremonial green tea with precise movements of a bamboo tea bowl, whisk, and tea scoop. I pick up the tea bowl, place it in my left palm, turn it ninety degrees, and sip. Its warmth travels down my throat, into my stomach, and blossoms revitalization into my soul. I bow gratitude to her.

We're sprawled under a plush blanket on the floor, graced by the warmth and glow of a wood-burning fireplace in a remote log cabin. There's no civilization in sight for miles, only snow and serenity. Rich kindling cedar envelops the darkness, and time does not exist.

I don't know how long it's been before my eyes open back to our apartment—seconds, maybe minutes—but I am renewed. Revived. *Healed,* even if just for a time.

"I adore you," I tell Casey.

She smiles back at me, and there's a twinkle in her eyes. "We're here, right now, and everything's okay."

2020-2021 was a dark, morbid time in many remarkable ways. I vividly remember the isolation. The day-to-day uncertainties. I don't remember feeling scared, but I could see palpable fear spreading like its own pandemic. The stress of trying to take care of my family while simultaneously serving in COVID-19 response operations

with the National Guard. Watching parts of American society collapse in ways reminiscent of Tommy Lee Jones' line from Men in Black: *"A person is smart. People are dumb, panicky, dangerous animals, and you know it." We worked so hard to find the little moments of joy and peace, ways to keep our heads above water long enough to take a breath before going under again. And we survived. That's what I'll always remember.*

OBSIDIAN GRACKLE

S AN ANTONIO — President Victoria Woodhull survived an assassination attempt today at approximately 1:14 p.m. shortly after disembarking Air Force One at Randolph Air Force Base, Texas.

In a joint statement, the White House and the Pentagon said that one Airman with the base's 902nd Security Forces Squadron has been detained in connection with the death of a Secret Service agent assigned to the president's security detail. The Pentagon did not name the Airman but did say the service member is currently undergoing evaluation by the Wilford Hall Medical Center Inpatient Psychiatry Flight at Lackland Air Force Base.

Neither agency revealed the homicide's connection to the assassination attempt, citing the ongoing investigation.

Day 1

It shouldn't be possible to fall asleep while marching, but I could do it a few paces at a time. All thirty-two of us in Flight 496 spent ridiculous amounts of time in Basic Training practicing marching in formation, stepping in endless circles around the parade grounds. Between our drill sergeant's hypnotic bellow of "*One, two, three, four!"* and San Antonio's blistering heat, I could even catch a few split-second dreams while my feet worked on autopilot. Thus, I wasn't entirely sure at first if I was dreaming or actually hearing the birds talk to me.

Chirp-chirp-chirp-chirp-chirp, screeeee, screeeee, blip-blip, blip-blip, chirp-chirp-chirp.

The big 'ole black blackbird's screeches and clicks sounded artificial. Robotic. Like a dial-up internet modem, but coming out of a living creature. I made the mistake of turning my head to birdcalls, lost my pacing, and marched right into the guy in front of me.

No, no, no, no, oh crap!

The unholy shadow of U.S. Air Force Staff Sgt. Jeremy Reynolds swooped in on me as I recovered, and the brim of his drill sergeant's Smokey Bear hat bounced off the side of my head as the flight and I continued forward perfectly in step. The outward composure required of me did not reflect the *please-just-kill-me-now* regret seizing my chest.

"Hey, crazy! Hey, crazy! What in the holy name of Hap Arnold are you looking at, Trainee Dawes? What's more flippin' pertinent than the back of your flipping fellow trainees' head while marching in the *position of attention?*" Staff Sgt. Reynolds screamed. His breath smelled so impeccably minty that my stomach lurched. It took everything to keep my face locked forward so that I didn't dare look away again.

"Sir, nothing, sir!"

"Then you must have *brain damage*! I didn't realize that *left-right-left* was going to be such a hardship for your handicapped sensibilities, you useless sack of numbnuts. Are the recruiters sending *brain-damaged* trainees to join the world's finest Air Force?"

"Sir, no, sir!"

"Flight, *halt!*" Staff Sgt. Reynolds called. The formation came to a crisp stop, and the drill sergeant propped himself inches from ear to whisper at me. Drill sergeant whispers were far worse than screaming. "Trainee Dawes, why are you here? If you want to get washed out, just say the word, and I'll make it happen right here, right now, no problem."

"Sir, no, sir! I'm here because I want to serve my country, sir!" I said.

Then the screaming resumed. "How about you start serving your country by mastering the simple act of *left-right-left*, you oxygen-wasting son of a *America's Got Talent* reject! *HUA!*" Staff Sgt. Reynolds hollered so loud that the entire flight's boots shook.

"Sir, yes, sir!"

"Trainee Dawes, step out of formation." I did. "Place your head between your legs." I did that, too. "Now say 'pop.'"

"Pop!"

"Louder, so Jesus can hear you!"

"*Pop!*"

"Do you know what that sound is?" Staff Sgt. Reynolds asked.

"Sir, Trainee Dawes reports as ordered: That's the sound of me pulling my head out of my ass," I said.

"*HUA!* So now, please ex[*cac-cac-cac-cac*] to me why you are *[blip-blip]*ing up my *[screeeeee]* formation, Trainee Dawes!"

Stress' adrenaline assured me I was awake, but I could've sworn that bird had just chirped over top the goliath voice of drill sergeant Staff Sgt. Reynolds.

"Sir: I'm confused at what you said, sir!" I said.

"*Holy [cac-cac-cac-cac]!* How many canteens of water have you had today, Trainee Dawes?" the drill sergeant demanded.

I tried to blink the salty sweat out of my eyes to see the bird behind Staff Sgt. Reynolds, sitting on the steaming blacktop a stone's throw away—large, slender, and obsidian black with neon yellow eyes. The great-tailed grackle—very common to the Lackland Air Force Base area, I would later learn. It looked right into me. Beckoning my attention. *Demanding* it.

"Sir... um--"

I couldn't focus on anything Staff Sgt. Reynolds said. Something emanated from that stupid bird like a magnetic radio wave, shooting right into my head. It twisted my vision, and the ground shifted under me until I had no choice but to grab Staff Sgt. Reynolds's arm for support.

"*Goddd* flippin' bless 'Merica!" Staff Sgt. Reynolds yanked another uniform out of formation. "Trainee Moussa, escort Trainee Dawes to sick call, and do not come back until he is rehydrated, miraculously healed of brain damage, or declared *[wheeeeeee]ing dead*!"

This is when I first learned of the obsidian grackle.

Day 8

The best duty assignment to get during Basic Training was "KP duty"—kitchen patrol. Sure, it meant working in the dining facility for fourteen hours straight, but we could eat as much as we wanted, and the drill sergeants didn't mess with us because they were too busy harassing the flights coming in for meals. Thus, no one would notice if I didn't come back inside right away from taking trash to the dumpster.

When I got outside, one of those robot-voiced grackles sat perched on top of the dumpster lid. I'd seen them more and more over the last week. I swear they were following me. This one was waiting for me to come outside. It didn't fly away when I got close. It wanted me to come closer.

"Hey there, fella," I said. "I need to get this trash in there."

The bird cocked its head, and its yellow eyes glowed fluorescent. *"Cac-cac-cac. Blip-blip, blip. Wheeeeeee. Cac-cac-cac-cac-cac."*

I felt tipsy suddenly, and it made me chuckle. "You sound like a computer."

"*Wheeeeeee. Cac-cac-cac-cac-cac.*" The grackle ruffled its feathers in what I thought might be irritation.

"Are you trying to tell me something?"

"Cac-cac-cac-cac. Blip-blip."

The grackle leveled its neon irises at me and beamed the invisible, magnetic bridge into my mind. The connection pummeled me on the forehead and paralyzed my body in the most hypotonic way, multitudes stronger in power than the experience on the parade field. It drowned out anything else around me. And then I could see something in my head. Letters. Numbers. Hazy at first, undefined in my mind's eye.

"Cac-cac-cac-cac. Blip-blip."

"'4b?' I don't know what that means," I mumbled. The black bird flapped its wings in a radiant outburst, and it jumped sense back into me. "Okay, okay!"

I regained the use of my hands and pulled out the notepad I was required to carry. I began writing the letters and numbers I heard in the pings, clicks, and whirls of the blackbird's call. The alphanumeric series scribbled in pen at the end of the bird's vocal volley read "4b696c6c."

I looked back to my grackle for any answer, but before I could ask, the dining facility backdoor swung open and clattered against the brick wall.

The bird startled and launched into the air.

"Dawes, what the hell are you doing? The dinner flights are about to come in. Let's go," Moussa said.

"Yeah... Sorry," I said, watching the bird escape into the distance.

4b696c6c. I could see and feel it with absolute clarity, yet I had no idea what the code meant. The crackle left me only with an undeniable sensation that it was a message delivered to me.

This is when I first learned the obsidian grackle was talking to me.

Day 27

The M16 rifle is a gas-operated, closed rotating bolt, semi-automatic rifle. It fires forty-five to sixty 5.56-millimeter NATO rounds per minute. It has a maximum effective range of 3,600 meters, with a point target range of 500 meters and an area target range of 600 meters. Do not point the barrel at anything you do not intend to shoot, maim, kill, or destroy. Keep your finger off the trigger and the safety on until you are ready to shoot. Treat all weapons as if they were loaded.

These were weapons specifications we were required to memorize and recite before rifle qualifications on the range—attention to detail, respect for the weapons system, so on and so forth.

I understood the fundamentals of shooting the rifle well enough: line up the front sight with the rear sight and slowly squeeze the trigger with the pad of your finger.

The pop-up targets were the problem. When they'd jump up, I'd flinch and squeeze too hard, throwing off my aim. I'd missed nine of the twelve so far, and Staff Sgt. Reynolds was not happy. The drill instructors weren't allowed to torment us while we were operating live weapons, but I could feel the frustration radiating off him, enough for me to stress even more. A few more missed shots, and they would recycle me backward a week or two in Basic Training or kick me out altogether. I wouldn't survive that.

And then, wouldn't you know it, one of those great-tailed grackles chose now—of all moments—to come over and harrass me.

The bird perched itself at the end of the firing range—abnormal because normally the gunfire would scare off any wildlife within earshot. I tried to ignore it, focusing downrange where the next pop-up target might jump.

"*Screeeee!*"

The grackle's screech surprised me, and I accidentally pulled the trigger. My shot hit a target square center mass, and it toppled over. *Perfect* timing.

"Finally! Nice shot, Trainee Dawes!" Staff Sgt. Reynolds hollered. "Whatever you did, do it again."

"*Chirp, screeeee, blip-blip, blip-blip.*"

I glanced over to my blackbird. It dipped its head to me, yellow eyes pulsating like a traffic caution light. I could see the letters and numbers in my head again, like my mind was automatically translating the bird's voice into alphanumeric code.

53686F6F74.

I put my attention back on the firing range and readied my rifle.

"53686F6F74!" the grackle screeched.

Okay, bird, whatever you say.

I pulled the trigger. Another perfect shot and the pop-up target toppled over.

"53686F6F74!"

Another target down.

"53686F6F74!"

Again.

"53686F6F74!"

Again.

"Holy mother of Moses, Trainee Dawes just decided to become a sharpshooter," Staff Sgt. Reynolds screamed. "Keep it up, and you're on track for the marksmanship ribbon!"

I emptied the magazine and slapped a new one into the rifle. Before releasing the bolt forward, I looked over to the bird and gave it a nod. I don't know if it could hear me, but I whispered "thank you" anyway. I owed it.

This is when I first learned to listen to the obsidian grackle.

Day 93

Most of my flight left Lackland Air Force Base for their tech school after graduating from Basic Training. The Air Force assigned me to the Security Forces career field, and that tech school was just a few blocks from the Basic Training dorms. My bus—a whole five-minute ride—left Flight 496 last, and I swear I saw tears of pride blossoming in Staff Sgt. Reynolds's eyes as we loaded up.

"See you in the field, crazies. *HUA!*" he said right before the bus doors closed.

Security Forces served as the Air Force's ground combat force and military police service, so the Security Forces Academy taught us many weapons and fighting skills, including rifle fighting techniques—using our rifles as striking devices. But since practicing with seven pounds of bayonet-equipped steel was a terrible safety hazard, we ran drills with pugil sticks. The foam-padded staff could still pack quite a wallop if wielded right, though.

A great-tailed grackle circled overhead one hot morning during rifle fighting practice, cheering me on with wild screeches and screams.

"*4B696C6C! 4B696C6C! 4B696C6C!*" over and over again.

Eventually, it became a distraction, and my sparring partner landed a solid slash right to the side of my head. I suppose the helmet provided some protection, but the crack and flash of light overtook me.

The next thing I saw was half my class and an instructor standing over me, beckoning me back to life. Their faces blurred in and out of triple vision.

"Can you hear me, Defender?" the instructor said, his words echoey and distant. "Can you tell me your name and rank?"

"Airman Basic," I muttered. "Andy Dawwww--" I rolled onto my side and upchucked my stomach contents onto the grass.

"Yep, that's a concussion," the instructor said.

I could still see the shadow of the black grackle gliding its circle around me in the sky, keeping its yellow eyes on me, still doing its job and broadcasting its message.

Which I could hear clearly now. Through the disoriented vision, the pain shooting down the skull, and sloshing nausea, I honed in my ears because I could listen to the bird differently now. The letters and numbers were replaced by plain English words in the same tone and pitch as the bird's robotic clicks and screeches.

"Kill! Kill! Kill!"

This is when I first learned to understand the obsidian grackle.

Day 110

Graduation day from the Security Forces Academy meant that we had crossed the threshold from being students to becoming active-duty Airmen. The next day, we'd all ship out to our first duty stations to start the rest of our lives, carrying everything we owned in the duffels across our backs. The last eighteen weeks of military indoctrination had been a fiery crucible designed to stress-test us until collapse, but we'd survived it. I'd survived it.

That night being our final night together, my class stuck our brand-new stainless-steel Security Forces badges in our pockets and celebrated at the base bowling alley with cheap beer and greasy pizza.

The news was ablaze about worldwide protests against the Saudi Arabian War. Apparently, something like 150,000 protesters had gathered in Washington, D.C., alone that day. "Blah, blah, blah," we spat back at the TV. But when President Woodhull came on-screen to make her statements, we cheered and toasted our pint glasses to her. Chances were that within a year, we'd all be deployed somewhere in the Middle East chasing down terrorists in the name of the Red, White, and Blue. "Bring it on," we said in our drunken stupors.

I did a shot with some girl, and we exited the bowling alley shortly after that for a smoke break—nothing like nicotine to chase down the booze. A great-tailed grackle sat atop the dumpster fence, waiting for me.

"Awww, come on, man, not tonight," I protested. "Can you give me a minute?" I asked the girl.

"But I thought we were coming out here for some privacy," she said.

"Just give me a minute!" I snapped back, and she sulked back inside.

I clicked my lighter several times—missing the cig several times thanks to the Earth's balance being off—until my smoke ignited. "Alright, just kidding. Whatcha got for me?"

"Kill the dragon! Kill the dragon!"

Something about the grackle's tone sobered me up faster than nature intended. This message felt different. Complete. Whole. Final. My smoke fell out of my mouth, but I couldn't bother picking it up.

"What the hell?" I asked. "What the hell's 'the dragon?'"

The bird flipped its head up several times, motioning behind me. I turned and saw the bar TV through the windows. The news replayed President Woodhull's remarks on the Invasion of Saudi Arabia campaign.

"Kill the dragon! Kill the dragon!"

I don't remember the rest of the night. I only remember those words echoing over and over. My first duty station was Randolph Air Force Base thirty-five minutes away, and I transferred there the next day with a good hangover. They had great-tailed grackles there, too. I saw the big black birds a good handful of times over the next year, just frequently enough to never let me forget. And they never said anything new.

The message never changed after that night at the bowling alley. It was always the same for the next five months, and it always seemed to show up alongside a mention of the U.S. president. It seemed conspicuously obvious.

Kill the dragon.

This is when I first learned the intent of the obsidian grackle.

But when the time came to "kill the dragon," would I be able to pull the trigger? What kind of mission did these obsidian grackles have me on? And, of course, the most obvious question: What if I was making this all up in my head?

I'm not. But what if?

Day 256

The Security Forces life at Randolph Air Force Base was more mundane than I imagined. I was one of the new guys, so all I did was check IDs at the Main Gate.

Twelve hours a day. Two days on, one training day, two days off. Rinse, repeat. Days, weeks, months.

Thankfully, my obsidian grackles were always there to keep me company.

There was a short time after I got to Randolph that I considered the talking blackbirds might have been a figment of my imagination, maybe hallucinations from the stress of basic training and tech school. I almost went to see Behavioral Health about it. Almost.

But my grackles appeared again shortly after I started working the graveyard shift—consistently delivering the same message but catching my attention at the correct times to keep me out of trouble with my sergeants. It couldn't be a coincidence. I even came to think of them as my good luck charm.

There were more grackles than usual flying around the base today. Today was my first presidential security detail. No complaints about working a twenty-hour shift; I always presumed it'd also be my last.

The Secret Service took the lead for presidential visits to the base, but my squadron—along with local law enforcement and FBI—would provide the extra security framework for a smooth visit. President Woodhull was in town to visit San Antonio for her re-election tour, so of course, she made time to shake the hands of veterans corralled behind a barricade along the flightline. Since the Security Forces Squadron had to be on duty for the distinguished visitor event, the consolation prize for us high performers was being paired up with interagency counterparts. That day, I got to work at a long-range observation post on top of one of the Randolph Air Force Base towers with a Secret Service Counter Sniper Team member.

My flight chief escorted me up the tower and introduced me to Stan.

"This is one of the 902nd's star performers, Airman Dawes," the flight chief said. "He's on track to get an M-4 designated marksman slot, so we thought he could shadow you today."

Stan did not extend a handshake. Stan seemed uneasy.

"Good to meet you," Stan said. The flight chief left us, and the countersniper eyeballed me. "Just do me a favor and keep your weapon on Safe and your barrel down, okay?"

"Sure thing," I said.

Stan didn't say much as he set up his gear and dialed in his scope. Some guys were just intense like that. Stan seemed to have a lot on his mind. I'd never met a Secret Service agent before. Maybe they were all like that.

Before too long, a single great-tailed grackle took its perch with us on top of the tower.

"Kill the dragon! Kill the dragon! Kill the dragon!" it screamed at me.

It was almost time. I was chatty and nervous, and I didn't care now if it made Stan uncomfortable.

"What are you zeroed in for?" I asked him, just out of occupational curiosity.

"200 meters," Stan said. His face reacted as soon as the sentence left his lips as if he had just disclosed classified information. Weird. "For close-quarter threats," he backpedaled.

"Cool," I said. Priming the rifle for that close of a distance didn't make sense, but I played it off like I was just happy to be there. Stan seemed to relax at my naïvete.

"Here, take a look," he said, handing me his spotting scope. It was nicer than anything we had in the unit, so I entertained myself by measuring out different points of the flight line. I noted that the barricades where the president would first shake veteran hands were almost precisely 200 meters out from our position. But I still noticed Stan texting on his cell phone out of the corner of my eye. I noticed because it was a flip phone, not a smartphone. Like a burner. The kind you threw away when you were done.

Air Force One landed some time later. My grackle didn't fly away from the noise of the Boeing 747. All the pomp and circumstance unrolled as planned, and before we knew it, President Woodhull was halfway from Air Force One to the barricades. I flipped on the M68 close combat optic on my rifle and discreetly looked down it to make sure I could see the red dot. The battery looked good. M9 pistol on my hip for backup. Ready to engage.

Stan looked at his flip phone one last time before putting it in his gear bag. He closed the bag up, and it flopped over, showing its front side. On it was an assortment of velcro patches—not uncommon for guys in our line of work to collect, but one, in particular, grabbed my attention. An exhale of relief ripped out of my lungs, and I almost had to turn away to collect myself before tears exploded from me. God bless those beautiful grackles.

Stan's nametag velcroed to his bag itself was not abnormal, but some of the consonants and vowels popped out at me most conspicuously.

"Wow. That last name's a mouthful," I said. "What is that, Polish? How do you pronounce that?"

Stan didn't look away from his scope. "*Druhs-gone-ski*. Drzazgownski. Everyone calls me 'Dragon' for short."

My eyes panned over to my obsidian crackle, and it screeched and thrashed its wings in a massive display of victory. I gave it a final nod. Of appreciation, I guess? Hindsight is very much twenty-twenty, but the grackles had always been diligent. Now I understood. Perfect hindsight. Clear direction.

President Woodhull was a half-dozen paces from the barricades. She already had her hands out to greet the first veteran. I'm sure Stan didn't think I noticed, but I watched him shift the safety off his rifle with his non-shooting hand.

"Hey, kid, do me a favor," Stan said. "My radio battery died." It hadn't. I could still hear unintelligible bits of radio chatter spilling out of his earpiece. "Can you go down and get another one out of the black suburban?"

I unlocked the safety of my hip holster, tightened my grasp around the pistol grip, and flipped the thumb safety back to "fire"—very slowly so Stan couldn't hear the clicks. He was so hyper-focused on his scope that I doubt he'd even realize if

I needed to chamber a round. Stan was sweating profusely, exhaling hard out of his nostrils. It was Texas hot, but not *that* hot.

"Sure thing, man," I said.

"Kill the dragon! Kill the dragon!"

"And could you get rid of that *[screeee]*ing bird while you're up?" Stan asked.

I pulled my pistol out of the holster and leveled it at the back of Stan's head.

"Absolutely."

This is when I first learned to obey the obsidian grackle. Surely, you must believe me now. Doesn't it all make sense?

"Obsidian Grackle" was first published in Mike Jack Stoumbos' Murderbirds: An Avian Anthology (Unhelpful Encyclopedia Vol. 1) *(WonderBird Press; April 21, 2023). Mike (also a Writers of the Future first place winner) is an incredibly gifted writer and talented publisher, who I first met at the Writers of the Future workshop in L.A. in 2022. It's been an absolute privilege to work for him on various projects, and he deserves every ounce of success he brings in. This story was inspired by the great-tailed grackles that inhabit the area of Joint Base San Antonio, Texas, where U.S. Air Force Basic Military Training is held. If you've ever heard these birds in nature—which, to me, sound like a dial-up internet modem—then you know why I had to write about them when Mike put out the call for bird-themed stories.*

OLD DEAN

Old Dean spent his old days staring out the windows of a nursing home. Most of them he lost the fight against his dementia, and the sun was setting on that lost battlefield. When snippets did come back here and there, it seemed to be feelings of regret. Or so he believed today.

Rusted but still running might have described his perpetual state of senility. Walking, but with a faulty compass. Lost. It was the same whether he was alone or having a visitor, like the sharp-dressed woman standing before him.

"Howdy," Old Dean said in that vintage Southern way.

"Good afternoon, Dean. Do you remember me from before?"

"I'm sorry," the old man said. "My noggin don't work so good anymore."

"That's okay, sir. My name is—" Dean immediately forgot it, but her voice was gentle and comforting. "I'm a cerebral archivist with the U.S. National Archives and Records Administration."

"Oh!" Dean didn't know what that meant, but it sounded significant enough for an impressed response.

"I'm here with good news," the archivist said.

"Oh yeah?"

"Yes, sir. We've selected your memories for holographic archiving. Your judiciary career was very significant in our nation's history. We want people to be able to experience your life virtually for generations to come."

"Oh." Dean winced. *Significant* didn't feel like a good fit for the blurry cloud where memory used to be. *Regrettable* did. *Empty*, too. "Well. When do you wanna do that?"

"The medical staff here have run a diagnostic on your genome terminus, and I'm afraid it'll have to be soon. I'm very sorry, Mr. Dean. There's just not much time left."

Silence fell upon them, punctuated only by the constant *tick... tick... tick...* of an antique analog clock clicking through the fog. Dean snapped his attention back to his guest when he realized he was drifting away, but he couldn't tell how many minutes or hours had passed. These were how his days went now.

"I just want to confirm; your file says there's no family we should contact?" the archivist asked.

"Nope. Just me," Dean said, staring back out the window again. He couldn't forget *that*. "Reckon I shoulda made time for a family."

Dean laid back in his bed—the best a legendary defense attorney's retirement could buy—and the archivist took care securing an apparatus around his head.

"This is gonna hurt," Dean said.

The archivist stopped to take a knee next to the bed.

"I *promise* you, this is completely painless," she said, her voice like a harp. "It'll be like watching an old film playing backward, very fast—your whole life, all in a matter of minutes."

"This is gonna hurt."

The archivist chalked it up to dementia, but Dean knew. Sometimes the pain of the mind was more excruciating than the body's.

"How's this doohickey work?" he asked.

"It uses quantum entanglement to transliterate your synaptic memories into digital data. Then we use four-dimensional mapping software to convert that data into a virtual, augmented reality for the museum."

"I don't think I know what that means," Dean said.

"It's okay, Mr. Dean. Neither do I. It just means it makes your memories so people can see them."

"But *why?*"

The archivist sensed the pained undertone in the question but didn't understand it.

"People appreciate history. 'To discover the constant and universal principles of human nature,' they say." The archivist made some final calibrations and stood before Dean with a remote trigger. "Alright, Mr. Dean, you just lay back and relax. I'll be right here when you wake up."

Dean's wrinkled eyes crested with tears, and the archivist knew something wasn't right. She'd completed this procedure dozens of times, but now some instinct prevented her thumb from pressing the remote. So instead, she walked over to hold his hand.

"Dean?" she asked. "What's your favorite memory?"

Old Dean took a moment to recall.

"Well... I suppose... I had me some waffles this morning. They warmed up the syrup and—"

The archivist pressed the trigger.

Dean's film accelerated backward from the present, too fast for him to fully make out. Only flashes and snapshots, some Dean didn't want to relive.

Alone in the nursing home. Silence. Stale air. The sun going down, the sun coming up. Over and over and over again.

A slip on the icy sidewalk that ended his independence.

The fruitless quest for meaning in retirement. No dollar amount could fly him somewhere where absolution awaited.

The country vacation lake where he realized his youth had escaped him forever.

The day he retired. Turning in the keys to the law firm—everything he had, everything he was—over in one simplistic moment.

Touching the keys of a grand piano in some lobby of some building somewhere, wishing he would have learned how to play when he was younger.

A news headline declaring, "Cuba Edgecomb executed for voluntary manslaughter."

Another saying, "Acquitted socialite arrested again."

Promotion to partner with the law firm. Through the celebration and neverending rounds of drinks, Dean remembered stifling a haunting suspicion that he hadn't found contentment.

Dean Parish—a.k.a. *The Jesus Christ of Criminal Defense*—representing Cuba Edgecomb on the (first) charge of homicide. Van Gogh used paint. Beethoven used a piano. Dean used reasonable doubt.

The intoxicating reputation of salvation for guilty clients.

Sacrificing *everything* to graduate law school *summa cum lade*.

One final brawl with his father before leaving for college. They never spoke again.

The fury of suffocating in claustrophobic adolescence.

Surviving every day to drown again the next.

Every spark that ever ignited a fight with—

Discord shook Dean's bones like a needle tripping across a vinyl record. He grit his teeth through the violent, disorienting skips of thrashing lights and nauseating motion until the film stopped and started playing in real-time. The memory was alive.

The low lights, long hallways, and smell of chemical sterility clued it to be a hospital. A young man leaned against an observation window separating the dark hallway from a nursery of newborns, his thousand-yard stare aimed at a single baby wrapped in a blue blanket. Dean would have recognized the stubbled face in the reflection, whether it was 30 or 50.

"Pa?"

The man flinched and turned away from the window.

"Yeah. I'm his pa."

The man's eyes simmered red with a hot glaze. It was about as much feeling as the hardened steel worker would allow himself.

"Where's his ma?" Dean asked although he thought he already knew the answer.

Dean's father clenched his teeth to force the words out. "She passed."

Dean hobbled over to join him at the window and peered at the innocent baby through his faded eyes. The newborn was so pure, untainted by any experiences to come. The child's entire life was in front of him, and it ignited a bitter fire deep inside Dean—a primal intensity to which he hadn't granted freedom in so long.

Dean fought through his mind's fog, turned to the man next to him, tightened his slack jaw, and mustered four words with as much clarity as he had felt in years.

"*It ain't his fault.*"

Pa's chin and lower lip shook. "I know it."

Then why'd you make me pay for it?

Dean collected every ounce of power in his husk of a body to lift his shaky, wrinkled hand and grab hold of the man's collar. He tried to make a fist and didn't care if slugging his dad broke every brittle bone in his hand, but arthritis wouldn't let him.

He slid his hand from his dad's collar to his shoulder. If time didn't grant him retribution, it might allow him obviation.

"You be real good to him, now. You're all the boy's got," Dean said, pointing a warped finger. He felt the sting in his own eyes, and his throat became tight, sending his voice soaring an octave. "Don't be too hard on him, y'hear?"

"I know it," his father said again.

"His ma had a piano, right?" Dean asked. "Let him play on it when he misses her and wonders what she was like."

Pa's strength collapsed, and he choked out sobs of pent-up grief and fear. Dean let him lean on him.

"Love him. Don't grudge him. Just love him," Old Dean said. "You promise it. *You promise it.*"

"I will." Pa slid against the wall to the ground and just cried. "I don't know what to do."

One of Old Dean's professors gifted profound encouragement to his first-year law students in the overwhelming face of learning the legal system.

"Just do what's *necessary*, Pa. Then do what's *possible*. Before you know it, you'll have done the impossible. Trust me. Works every time."

Dean was no longer staring at newborns through a window but at a pair of youngsters staring back at him in the room of his mediocre nursing home, the best a third-generation steelworker could afford.

"Hi, Papa! Hi, Papa!"

"Where'd that lady go?" Dean asked.

"Who, Dad? Your nurse?" a man and a woman asked from across the room.

"The archivist. She was downloading my memories."

The couple exchanged looks. Dean knew what it meant; his noggin didn't work so well anymore. But surely he hadn't imagined the archivist?

"Papa, there wasn't anyone else here," Dean's daughter-in-law said.

"She said I was going to pass soon."

"Hey, Dad, don't talk like that. You've got plenty of gas left in your tank," Dean's son lied.

Dean tested the theory and dug deep into his memory for any shred of proof. Then, finally, he grabbed hold of a little something and grinned.

"*Mutatis mutandis*. It means 'once the necessary changes have been made,'" he announced.

"That's great, Dad," Dean's son said. "Did you hear that on one of the court shows on TV?"

Dean didn't answer but just sat back and smiled. He remembered.

"Papa! Papa! Play us a song," the children begged.

Were these his grandchildren? Dean reckoned he'd never seen two more beautiful little cherub faces.

"A song?" Dean asked. "Oh, sweetpeas, I don't know how—"

"Go ahead, Dad," Dean's son said. "Play that bluesy one the kids love. Remember it?"

Dean's son pulled a harmonic out from the dresser drawer, and the children brought it to Old Dean. The faithful aroma of old brass and maple fired up his smoldering memory, and his palms curled around it like a hug. He knew the music, even if he forgot every once in a while.

Old Dean spent his old days staring out the windows of a nursing home. Most of them he lost the fight against his dementia, and the sun was setting on that battlefield. But, when he could remember, it seemed to be recollections of warmth. Or so he believed today.

"Old Dean" was first published in HyphenPunk Magazine #9 *(HyphenPunk; September 4, 2023). I wrote this story after finding a photo of my grandfather holding my infant firstborn child. The photo captures Grandpa looking at the camera with this ever-so-slight smile and wide-eyed look that I knew was the joy of him holding his first grandchild. The juxtaposition of old and new fired up this idea of, "What would it be like to hold your baby-self as an old man?" Although the pictured scene didn't make it into the final draft, the concept of "what we leave behind and why" stayed prominent.*

PARANORM

S pirits don't make shadows, so Rosie Wildes didn't realize one was following her until she turned around and just about walked over the translucent little boy. She shrieked, and the ashen child recoiled as startled toddlers do. His mouth melted into the deep frown that precedes thick tears.

"Oh no, baby, it's okay," Rosie said, swallowing her terror. Seeing a ghost—no matter its disposition—was always unnerving. She kneeled on the interstate gravel and held her arms out. "I'm sorry. I didn't mean to scare you. It's okay."

The boy sniffed back his tears and inched forward. The closer he got, the more saturated his color became, and soon he transformed from a grayscale spirit to almost real-life colors. "*I sorry,*" he echoed.

Federal Bureau of Investigation Special Agent Saul Jarad watched from a cautious distance with his MiniDV camcorder rolling. Judging by Rosie's conversation with nothingness, it was a reasonable assumption that his confidential informant had made contact with something else.

The nervous ghost child stopped just out of Rosie's arm's reach and held his hands up to his mouth.

"My name's Rosie. What's yours?"

"*Mi-cuhl.*"

"Michael? Are you lost, honey?"

The boy nodded.

"Okay. Well, you can stay with me as long as you want to, all right?" The boy nodded again and lowered his hands. "Where's your mommy and daddy, Michael?"

"*I dunno. Daddy's sad. He's crying.*"

"Why is he sad?"

"*I dunno.*"

"Hey. Would you like a sucker?"

Michael surrendered a grin, and Rosie manifested an orange lollipop to hand him. The ethereal illusion did the trick, and the child moseyed over and nested up to Rosie. She gave him a tight hug, and his energy almost felt real in her arms.

"A Caucasian boy, just a preschooler, maybe four or five. Dark brown hair, medium crew cut. Fair skin, grayish-blue eyes," Rosie told Saul, who had crept close enough to get within earshot with the camera's audio. "Blue pajama shorts, white pajama top with a blue baby shark on it. No shoes."

She choked on the tightening in her throat.

"He's hurt. Long bruises on the right side of his face and arm, left side of his neck." The more she observed, the more the injuries appeared. "His right eye has blood in it. Shoulder is out of the socket. Maybe a broken leg. *Jesus, god.*"

"Keep going, keep going," Saul whispered.

"No, I can't. No, no, *no.*" Rosie clenched her eyes shut.

"*What's the matter?*" Michael asked.

Anxiety seized Rosie's ability to breathe. "I'm sorry. I'm sorry," she wheezed. Rosie waved her hands frantically in an enchanted gesture that caused the boy to vanish away like smoke in the wind. She scrambled away from Saul's aid and charged into the Nevada field, away from the scene, away from the overbearing sensations of death. Saul lit a menthol cigarette and used the downtime to review the video footage, memorizing every detail of Rosie's narration.

Rosie came back infuriated.

"I'm not doing this," she said. "Turn me over to the Feds, I don't give a shit. I am—"

"It's an astral echo, not a ghost," Saul said. "He didn't die here. They didn't find a child's body, so it's not a ghost. It may not even be real."

"*So what?*"

"That manifestation is the *only* link we have to the suspect right now. If it's an echo, it's tied to the killer's state of mind," Saul said. Rosie responded with silence. Receptive silence. "It's our only lead."

"What now, then?" she asked after the lull.

"If I'm right about the shooter's position, that echo will reappear on that overpass." Saul pointed to where the West Rose Creek Road crossed Interstate 80 half a mile down the road. "It won't remember the conversation you just had. So, press for different details."

Rosie stared into the distance and considered the theory.

"Look, if I'm wrong, you're off the hook, job done," Saul said. "If I'm right, maybe we get one more step in the right direction. Please, Rosie. I can't do this without you. You know I can't."

27 Hours Earlier

Earl J. Taggert died at sunrise on October 2, 1997—a peaceful fall morning in rural Nevada, orange hues kissing hilly grassland all the way down I-80. The interstate was flat and straight, his 18-wheeler was running faithful at 80 miles per hour, and an old-time country music station was coming in well enough on the AM radio. All was right in the world.

Everything went wrong when he first heard the little boy's voice.

Strong static and a pitchy, oscillating whine overtook the CB radio, punctuated with a few almost-tangible words.

"...daddy...gonna hurt..."

Earl flipped off the music, afraid his old ears were playing tricks on him.

"...sorry...my daddy..."

No, that was real.

"EJ Nevada, break, break. Say again, handle. You're coming in broken. Did you say someone's hurt?"

"EJ Nevada, EJ Nevada, this is Reno Hal, Reno Paravestigations," another CB'er said. *"I'm detecting a white noise frequency on this channel. What do you hear?"*

"Emergency traffic, clear channel one-niner. I think there's a little kid in trouble on the CB," Earl said. He didn't have much patience for crackpots jamming up the airwaves.

"Copy. I'm only picking up the white noise. Standing by for assistance."

The channel cleared to nothing but the static and pitchy whine wavering up and down.

"Kid, you there?" Earl asked.

"I sorry, my daddy..." More static. It was the wee chirping of a toddler's voice.

"I can't hear you, kiddo. Is your daddy hurt?"

The static grew louder, and the pitch skyrocketed higher and higher, until it all snapped to crystal clarity.

"I sorry. My daddy's gonna hurt you."

Those words froze Earl in utter, chilled perplexity and he just stared at the radio. He keyed up his mic but didn't know what to say.

"I sorry. My daddy's gonna hurt you."

That voice came from the passenger seat. The boy had dark hair, pale skin, bright eyes. Maybe four years old. He wasn't translucent, but wasn't there, either. Earl was a simple salt-of-the-earth kind of man. He was grateful for what the Good Lord provided him and tried to not pay much heed to anything beyond that. Sure, he had seen a handful of strange things in four decades of trucking, but this defied it all.

Earl felt no panic, no horror. Just unadulterated confusion. He side-eyed his new passenger while white-knuckling the steering wheel with one hand and crushing his CB microphone with the other—then realizing he'd been broadcasting the whole time.

"I... I, uh... I think I just seen a ghost."

The little boy fastened the passenger seatbelt across himself.

"EJ Nevada, Reno Hal: Can you give a description of the apparition? Is it posing a threat?"

"I sorry." The boy grinned, as if he were proud he could articulate an apology. His parents must've been practicing manners with him.

He felt it before he heard it, but that's when a gunshot ended Earl.

The single bullet crushed through the semi's windshield and ripped through his flannel shirt, just above the sternum. Earl always presumed it was a heart attack that would take him to heaven's pearly gates. As he slumped forward into the steering wheel, he imagined the lead-induced burning and pinching in his chest was what one might have felt like.

Earl fought to shuffle his foot onto the brake and leaned right onto the wheel to guide the semi onto the shoulder in his final semi-conscious moments, refusing to let his truck become a road hazard.

Earl had already passed away when the tractor jackknifed into the trailer and sent the entire rig tumbling. Sparks turned engine fluids into flames, and Earl and his crumpled rig were smoking charcoal by the time the firefighters and ambulances arrived.

Earl in Nevada wasn't the first, but law enforcement didn't connect him to the handful of other assassinated truckers after his complicated autopsy. Not until the case landed on the desk of Saul Jarad at the Federal Bureau of Investigation's Las Vegas field office.

"Jarad! Did the doc clear you back to duty?" Division Chief Mitcher bellowed from across the office.

Saul looked up from his stack of files like a kid caught in the cookie jar. He could hide his bruised hands in bandages, but not two raccoon-like black eyes.

"Yes, sir, just today."

"I want to see the release," Mitcher said. "Where's your case at?"

"Wrapped. I'm about to forward everything to the district attorney today."

"Good. Give it to someone else. You're up. Trucker and his rig barbequed on the interstate, all you."

Mitcher tossed a packed manila folder onto the desk.

"Winnemucca is asking for help. The driver took a long-range round to the chest, made a big boom-boom, and the scene's getting cold," Mitcher said.

"Highway Patrol can't handle a shooting, boss?" Saul asked, thumbing through the file.

"There's no ballistics. No bullets, no casings, no powder. It's a magic J-F-friggin-K bullet—got paranorm written all over it. The only good lead is maybe an EVP recording off the CB radio from a local."

Mitcher pointed his finger at Saul's face to indicate the official order. "I want you up north by *tonight*."

"Sure thing, Chief."

Mitcher took out several pieces of gum and flung them at Saul.

"That garlic is seeping out your goddamn bones."

"Garlic's cheaper than silver bullets, boss. Plus, you know I can't give up the Chinese food. Don't ask me to do that, please, Chief, I'm begging."

A cubicle away, Saul's senior partner, Special Agent Julianne Mueller, muzzled a snicker. It alerted Mitcher, and he zeroed in on her.

"And *you*. Stop burning through so many rounds, Mueller. Silver's expensive as *shit*. Fiscal year just started, and you're already two magazines in the hole. Keep it up, and it's coming out of your paycheck."

Julianne threw her hands up in protest. "*Chief!*"

"$4.60 an ounce, Annie Oakley!"

"It's okay, Chief," Saul said. "I'll just teach her some of my boxing moves."

Mitcher evaluated Saul's battered face, growled, and moved on.

Saul smiled, packed up his previous case, and opened the new file for a better look. Being sidelined had him sick with cabin fever, and he was glad to be back. He was built for fieldwork. And ever since Reagan passed the Abnormal Entity Act of 1981, the FBI's Behavioral Analysis Unit 6 had never been short of assignments in the counter-paranormal operations department.

"You know, you still owe me for the lycan," Julianne said.

"What are you talking about? I had him on the ropes."

"*Please.* Your face would've been a smashed pumpkin—"

"Love that band."

"—if I hadn't unloaded on that perp. I don't know what Mitcher's complaining about. A body bag's cheaper than incarceration."

"That's not very nice, Agent Mueller."

Saul's smile faded a few pages into the file.

A Class 8 semi-trailer truck.

Emerald green.

"Dammit," he muttered. He stood up and whipped on his blazer.

"What's wrong?" Julianne asked.

"Could you do me a favor and run a ViCAP report on incidents involving Class 8 and 9 semi-trucks this year, please? Single-vehicle ones, with driver fatalities?"

"Sure," Julianne said. "Where are you going?"

"I need a haircut."

The mall was mostly empty, the same as the chairs in the salon, so Rosie should have been glad to have a customer on a dead Friday morning. The other hairstylists wouldn't be in until the afternoon traffic picked up, so the pre-lunch shift was all hers. Special Agent Jarad, however, was the last person she wanted to see.

She crossed her arms, planted a hip, and let her eyes shoot daggers. "What do *you* want?"

Saul held his arms out in feigned offense.

"Rosie! Can't a guy get a haircut?"

He always kept it trimmed short—a one-length, do-it-yourself, bachelor cut. A Number 4 clipper comb, if Rosie had to guess. This one looked to be only about two weeks old.

"What am I supposed to do with that?" she asked.

"High and tight, please. Nice and easy. I'll tip good, promise."

His boyish charm and whiskey-smooth voice were disarming. It's probably why he was a good investigator.

"Shut up and sit down," Rosie said.

"Yes, ma'am."

Rosie whipped a cape around him and snapped a Number 0 comb on her clippers.

"Why are you here?" she asked. She ran the clippers across the sides of his head, flinging little clumps of hair onto the floor. The faster she cut, the sooner he'd leave.

"Just a hunch. I need your expertise on a case."

"I can't keep doing this, Saul," Rosie said. "I missed a lot of work this year. People noticed."

"That's our arrangement, Rosie, which I—for the record—am truly grateful to you for."

Rosie thrust the clippers up the back of Saul's head and hoped it hurt as much as the fact that she agreed to be a confidential informant to keep the Department of Justice off her back.

"And, what, you will personally burn me at the stake the day I say 'no'?"

Saul rarely lowered his happy-go-lucky guard, so Rosie knew he was serious when he put his hand on hers and locked eyes in the mirror.

"I would never do that, Rosie."

His stone expression did not waver, and he refused to break the gaze. She conceded and swiped away a single mascara-thickened tear from the corner of her eye. She knew he'd never turn her over. Saul was a good friend. But the daily stressors of hiding in plain sight in don't-ask-don't-tell America—always having to look over her shoulder to see who was giving her magic a second glance—was suffocating.

"What do you want?" Rosie switched to a bigger comb to blend the high into the tight.

"I've got a hot crime scene. Paranorm. Looks like an untraceable bullet, and maybe some recorded Electronic Voice Phenomena. That's all we've got. I need you to take a look at the scene and tell me anything you can. We just need to be pointed in the right direction, that's all."

Rosie continued buzzing in silence, thinking it over.

"I think he'll kill again. And has before," Saul added after a reluctant pause. "I feel a hunch on this one."

"Jesus. Where?"

"Seven hours north. We'll need to be there by tonight."

"Saul!"

"I'll buy you a nice dinner, promise," Saul said. "And you'll save lives. That's a good thing to do, right?"

Rosie brushed the clippings off his head, unsnapped the cape, and let out a defeated sigh.

"I can't leave until three. Just pick me up here. I still have my go-bag in the car."

"Are you off tomorrow?"

"I guess I am now."

Saul slapped his hands together and let out a big grin. "*Yes*, that's my Rosie. How much do I owe you for the cut?"

"$60."

Saul paused mid-reach for his wallet.

"Geez. That's a little steep, isn't it?" he asked.

Rosie held her hand out with a vindictive smirk.

"That's just a down payment to cover tomorrow's missed work. You know it's not cheap to hire a witch."

"There are 134 hits on file year-to-date," Julianne said when Saul walked back into office. She already had a map on the corkboard pierced with multicolored thumbtacks shotgunned across the nation with no geographic logic. Saul lost no time fixating on them.

There was an old wives' tale that you could stop a vampire dead in its tracks by throwing a bunch of something in front of it. It'd have to count every item before continuing an attack, thanks to the vampire's arithmomaniac nature.

Likewise, if you wanted to stop Saul Jarad, just put a forensic equation in front of him that needed solving. It was his nature to solve crime.

"Want to narrow the parameters?" Julianne asked.

"Very much," Saul said, without looking away from the map.

"Where do you want to start?" Julieanne asked.

"Were there any obvious correlations?"

Julianne flipped through her stacks of files again. "Nothing obvious. Different companies, different homes of record, different cargo, different drop-off points."

Saul's eyes darted from tack to tack, variable to variable, and the cogs in his mind started heating.

The search for order.

The search for order.

Saul gave up, lit a cigarette, and blew the minty smoke at the map. He had that one hunch, something that itched the back of his mind from the beginning, but it was a stretch.

"How many of them were emerald green?" he asked.

"What's emerald green?"

"It's a shade of green."

"The truck or trailer?"

"Just the truck," Saul said. "Trailers change."

Julianne punched away at her desktop's keyboard. "Four."

"All in the Mountain West region?"

Julieanne flipped through the files.

"Idaho, two in Nevada. The latest was outside Salt Lake City. All open cases labeled probable homicides. What the hell?"

Perhaps the order was found.

"Ballistics?"

"All inconclusive, but indicative of long-range." She looked up at Saul.

"It's the same guy," Saul said. "Remember that drug trafficking case we closed out a few months back? That junkie trucker with the burns? He kept saying, 'Kill emerald green,' over and over. I remembered it when I read this case. Four homicides this year, all in our backyard, all involving emerald green trucks and long-range shootings? Tell me that's not something."

"Saul, he was blitzed on PCP. He didn't even know what he was saying."

"And yet, a correlation." Saul's instinct was quickly evolving into a conviction. "Tell me about the witness in Winnemucca."

"A local ham radio operator was running recording hardware. Says he's got the whole incident and an authentic EVP on tape."

"Sounds like a solid starting point," Saul asked.

Julianne let out a vexed sigh and rubbed her forehead. "It's Kooky Hal."

"Paranormal investigator Kooky Hal?"

"*Amateur* paranormal investigator."

Saul raised an eyebrow. "Jealous that someone is hogging your turf?"

"Please."

"Okay. How about I take the one in Winnemucca. I'll pick Hal's EVP on the way up. You take Salt Lake City, and we'll see where it goes from there?" Saul asked.

"How about we *both* take Winnemucca and Salt Lake City?" Julieanne's candor could always be counted on to float the unsaid to the surface.

"I gotta bring my C.I. in on this one, Julieanne. I just have a feeling."

"For chrissake, Saul. You know, it's a little screwed up that you have an informant you keep from your partner."

"I know, Julieanne. I'm sorry. You just gotta trust me. It wouldn't be safe."

"For *who*?"

"For either of you."

Saul planted himself at the ashtray outside the mall entrance a little before 3 p.m., having traded his suit and tie for comfortable jeans and a T-shirt for the long drive. His work sedan sat waiting in the fire lane when Rosie left the mall right on time with her go-bag slung over her shoulder. She walked past him and jumped into the passenger seat without saying a word. Saul flicked his cigarette butt away and plopped into the driver's side.

"All set?" Saul asked, hoping for optimism. He loved a good road trip.

"It's not like I have a choice," Rosie said.

"There's always a choice, Rosie."

Saul put the car in gear and headed for U.S. Route 95 North. The road was dry and flat, hypnotic. Saul had almost fallen catatonic to it before realizing Rosie was eyeballing the steering wheel. It was his trademark fingerless tactical gloves, the ones with carbon fiber knuckles. A warm October day in the high 80s was hardly glove weather.

"Why do you always wear those?" Rosie asked.

Saul looked at her with an ornery smile.

"They're my driving gloves. Secret weapon."

"Whatever."

"Speaking of secret weapons," Saul reached into the center console and pulled out an envelope thick with cash. "Here is your fee and per diem."

Rosie took the envelope, hid it in her purse, and sat in silence. After a few uncomfortable moments, Saul turned on the radio, which was still on the local talk radio station.

"—to say, paranorms are not natural. Look at Lying Lilith, the first to disobey God in the Garden of Eden, now a baby-stealing night demon. Look at Killer Cain, the first murderer, now cursed to wander the Earth undead, soulless, forever. Since the beginning of time, God has hated paranormal entities. Thank God our government—"

Saul flipped the radio as fast as he could, but a few seconds of political venom was a few seconds too much. He could see Rosie's eyes brimming with hot tears.

"Sorry about that," Saul said. Rosie remained silent as she gazed out the window. "So... Got any plans for Halloween?"

Rosie turned to him and glared.

"What?" he asked.

"I don't have any hot tips for the Limen, if that's what you're asking."

"That's not what I'm asking."

"I'm not going to help you kill whatever crosses through the portal. I've told you over and over, I will not hunt other paranorms."

"Damn, Rosie, I just wanted to know what you're dressing up as. Honest."

Rosie sulked down into the passenger seat.

"I don't dress up," she said. "I hand out candy and put protection blessings on the kids."

"That's very kind."

"Not all paranorms are evil, you know. We shouldn't all have to hide because of the bad ones."

Saul took her hand and gave it a good squeeze.

"Why do you think I look out for you?" he asked.

"Because you can't solve your own cases."

"Well... uh, sure. But also because good people like you are a candle on the world's path of darkness and fear. That's what my grammy used to say."

"I wish more people felt that way," Rosie said.

"Someday, Rosie. Someday."

Reno was a solid detour to the west, but it'd be well worth it if the EVP tape panned out. Kooky Hal's base of operations was in an urban residential area, but his homemade fortifications made it look like a militia's compound.

Saul parked on the street and handed Rosie his cellphone.

"What's this for?" she asked.

"You'd better hang back. Kooky Hal is a bit of an... extremist. Just page me if something comes up."

Saul guessed ringing the doorbell wasn't necessary, judging by the overabundance of security cameras, but he did anyway out of courtesy. The door's sliding peephole racked open to reveal thick glasses and a burly beard to match the untamed hair of a crazy man. Saul pulled out his identification.

"Special Agent Jarad, FBI, here about your EVP recording."

"Teeth."

Saul exposed his pearly whites. No fangs.

"Eyes."

Kooky Hal showed an ultraviolet light across Saul's face. No concealer contacts.

"Blood. Hold out your right index finger."

Saul complied, and Kooky stuck him with a spring-loaded lancet. Saul watched through the peephole as Kooky took the blood sample to a glass slide, sprinkled a shimmering powder onto it—salt, ash, garlic, and silver, Saul guessed—and slid the glass under a microscope.

"No necrosis," Kooky said when he returned to the door. His demeanor had become more amenable. "You're not paranorm."

"Thanks for the tip."

"Can't be too careful these days. Who knows how many of them are walking among us, y'know?"

"You have something for me?"

"*Oh* yeah," Kooky promised. He unbolted the door and swung it open. "You're going to love this."

Kooky led Saul to his workstation, where he had software and an audio waveform keyed up on a computer screen.

"This is what I pulled off the CB yesterday," he said.

"Emergency traffic, clear channel one-niner. I think there's a little kid in trouble on the CB."

"Copy. I'm only picking up the white noise. Standing by for assistance." That was Kooky Hal's voice.

"Kid, you there?"

Static.

"I can't hear you, kiddo. Is your daddy hurt?"

More static. A high-pitched whine going higher and higher until gone.

"I sorry. My daddy's gonna hurt you." That was a child's voice.

Kooky stopped the audio and looked for Saul's reaction with a giant grin.

"So, that's the EVP?" Saul asked.

"No. *No. That's* the thing. I couldn't pick up any of what EJ Nevada was hearing on the other end of his channel. It was all static. That child's voice, that was organic. *That* was the apparition *in* the truck with him, *right* before it all got messy."

Saul didn't quite know what to think yet. "Creepy," he said.

"You think that's creepy? *Here's* your EVP."

Kooky isolated the last piece of static on a loop so it repeated over and over again. He applied several audio restoration and compression filters and adjusted the equalization frequencies until almost discernible sounds began to come through.

"Help, please. My son. Please. Michael."

The man's voice sounded distorted, raspy. Desperate. It melted away to a different, granular, deep voice. It was dark, inhuman, unnerving—the sensation you feel at the back of your skull when you know you're in danger. It upset Saul's gut more than he wanted to admit.

"Intervene. Kill emerald green."

"Now, what do you think *that* means?" Kooky asked.

The recording stopped and Saul realized he could breathe again. He forced out a few exhales, just to be sure.

"Well, Hal, for now that means I'm going to need a copy of those tapes."

The crime scene was about nine miles from Saul and Rosie's motel down Interstate 80, just west of the municipal airport. Earl's truck slid far enough off the road to impede only one of the westbound lanes, and the traffic was light enough that the Highway Patrol could divert the cars around the smoldering mess. At their current position, it was 15 miles of flat grasslands in any direction with no cover or concealment until reaching the mountains, some of which towered up to 9,400 feet.

The initial ballistics report indicated a perpendicular, high-elevation shot by something in the ballpark of a 7.62-millimeter NATO round. Therefore, an approximate maximum effective range of between 800 and 1,000 meters. All that to say it pointed to an improbable—hell, *impossible*—sniper shot, even with a magic bullet. Except for—

"Are you much into sport shooting, Rosie?" Saul asked.

"No." She sounded offended.

"There's only one possible place the shot could've come from." Saul pointed east, to the West Rose Creek Road overpass half a mile away, the one they had driven under on the way over.

"How the hell do you figure that?"

"I did six years with the Army while I was working on my bachelor's degree. Had a lot of trigger time on the ranges. Combat in Grenada and Panama. Based on everything I've ever learned about shooting, *that's* the perch. The sun would've been at the shooter's back. High ground with the rig right ahead. The overpass' railing for a supported position. Perfect, really."

"But it's so far away."

"Not for someone who knows what they're doing. Someone planned this." The more Saul evaluated the landscape, the firmer his instincts felt. "You're up," he told Rosie. "I need you to read this scene, see what the rest of us can't see."

"I'll need the area cleared so I can work," Rosie said.

"No problem." Saul called over the handful of Highway Patrolmen to brief them, and they soon sauntered away.

The crime scene felt empty to Rosie. She couldn't sense any energies swirling around, good or bad. Perhaps too much time had passed since the crash. She pulled out a tape recorder and headphones to listen to Kooky Hal's recording while circling the smoldering wreckage.

"Kid, you there?... I can't hear you, kiddo. Is your daddy hurt?"

"I sorry. My daddy's gonna hurt you."

"'I'm sorry. My daddy's gonna hurt you,'" Rosie whispered. She tried to hone in on the words, the tiny voice, the energy of the moment. Finding it, *feeling* it, beckoning it closer. "'I'm sorry. My daddy's gonna hurt you.'"

Spirits don't make shadows, so Rosie didn't realize one was following her until she turned around and just about walked over the translucent little boy.

"Look, if I'm wrong, you're off the hook, job done," Saul said. "If I'm right, maybe we get one more step in the right direction. Please, Rosie. I can't do this without you. You know I can't."

Rosie fumed heavy breaths of terror and anger, and Saul did feel sharp remorse for backing her into a corner. He tried to repress his guilt with the reminder that his arrangement with Rosie was leveraged to save lives.

Rosie's eyes darted back and forth from the overpass to Saul and back again.

"Let's get this over with," she eventually said.

Saul confirmed with the Highway Patrol that they had not yet examined the overpass before he and Rosie left one crime scene for what Saul suspected was another. He knew they were in the right spot when Rosie gasped on approach. With her third eye, she could see what was hidden before.

"What do you see?" Saul asked.

"Colors," Rosie said. "Like an aura, but it's just hanging in the air, like fog. Barely there. It's beautiful."

"Read it. What do the colors mean?"

"Lots of dark reds, with grays and blacks," Rosie said. "Fear and anger. And indigo? Like a mix of blue and purple. I don't know what... It feels like psychic energy. Fury and healing. Contradictory. It doesn't make sense."

"No, that's great, Rosie. Good work."

A forensics team would use a chemical test to identify any nitrate residue left behind from gunpowder in a typical crime scene. But, as Saul and Rosie already knew, this was no normal crime scene. Instead, Saul jumped out of the car, fired up the Kirlian energy counter from his field kit, and began waving the wand throughout the scene until the machine started humming at energy detections, right up against the railing facing the oncoming traffic. He pulled out his tape recorder and hit record.

"October 3rd, 1997, 1:55 Zulu, at the suspected shooter's perch, West Rose Creek Road at I-80, in Winnemucca. Approximately 27 hours from the time of incident. Initial energy reading is 1.2 Kirlian-hertz."

"What's that mean?" Rosie asked.

"With this reading and knowing the event time, we should be able to get an idea where the activity originated from."

"You're kidding. What kind of idea?"

"I'm no mathematician, but with this reading at 27 hours, I'd guess something like a 400-mile radius."

"Geez. That's a lot of radius," Rosie said.

"That's where you come in. Press the echo for something geographical. Anything more specific."

Immersing into the corona of the astral plane—the spirit world—felt like sinking back into a cushy chair of cold steam. Once Rosie could slow her mind to a crawl and focus energy to her spirit, the hidden realm enveloped her. The air became thicker, more conductive to everything around her. When she opened her eyes on the overpass, she saw the vivid aura fog more clearly, and this time Michael was waiting under the umbrella glow of its luminance.

"Hello. My name's Rosie. What's yours?"

"*Mi-cuhl.*"

"Are you lost, Michael?"

The boy nodded, again.

"Well, that's okay. I can help you get home. What's your address?"

Michael shrugged. *"I hadda go to da hops-pit-tul. Daddy's sad."* The long bruises on his face and arm started to form, and he winced.

Rosie fought back the tightness growing in her chest with focused breaths, but with no promises for how long her resiliency would hold up.

"Michael, I have a mobile phone in the car. What number are you supposed to call when you're lost?"

The toddler perked up as his working memory kicked into gear. *"Fife-fife-fife, two-one, two-sicks, that's my phone number and it sticks."*

"That's a good rhyme. Do you know what state we're in?"

"Yeah! Utah."

Rosie could feel Saul scurrying in the background.

"I need a name and address trace for 801-555-2126... Yep, got it."

"Hey! Look at dis." Michael snatched Rosie's hand and pulled her down the overpass, away from the aura glow. His injuries were still beginning to manifest, but he didn't seem to actually notice yet. He stopped at the shoulder and pointed down to the sediment. Rosie could see part of a hollow brass cylinder enveloped in faint a blood-red glow poking up through the mix of silt and litter. *"Look. It's pretty."*

She struggled to identify the artifact, but had worked with Saul enough times to know not to touch evidence. "What is it?" Rosie asked the toddler.

Saul swooped out of nowhere, poked a pen into the silt, and lifted the brass out of the dirt with it. Rosie lost concentration and Michael vanished.

"*That* should not exist," he said, examining the metal in the sunlight. "It's a 7.62-millimeter casing. A very *real* leftover from our magic bullet."

"I don't understand. How?" Rosie asked.

"Magic bullet, real casing, and that energy aura? I think we've got ourselves a genuine kinetic portal generation. Real gun, real bullet, magic energy projection. Now, the question is, who's on the other side?"

It was five hours due east to Salt Lake City, the metropolitan focal point where Michael's telephone number registered and where Special Agent Mueller was already investigating one of the related trucker incidents. Saul had abandoned the idea of coincidences early in his career, so he put in the call to Julieanne as soon as he and Rosie vacated their motel.

"What have you figured out over there?" he asked.

"*Squat. Long-haul trucker with a headshot from a big boy rifle, but zero on ballistics. And I mean absolutely* nothing. *I think we're looking at kinetic bullet projection here.*"

"Agreed," Saul said. "I think I've got something. We're on our way to you. Should be there by 4 p.m."

"*We?*"

Think fast, think fast.

"I've got a Bureau specialist with me. We've got some physical evidence for Salt Lake's lab and maybe a name and address on the suspect. Can they have their SWAT team ready to go when we get there? I don't want to take any risks with this guy."

"*Good deal. Yeah, I'll make the call right now. What are we looking at?*"

"Pure speculation, but with what we've got so far, I'm guessing a paranoid psychosis. There's no common denominator with the victims that makes sense except those green trucks."

And nothing would make any more sense when the trio met at the modest house registered to 555-2126. Julieanne made it there first and waited a block down the road, leaning against her rental with a cup of coffee.

"That's your partner?" Rosie asked. "She's cute."

"Not your type."

"And what do you know about 'my type,' Saul?"

"She's, uh, well... She's not fond of paranorms," Saul said.

"Oh."

Julieanne greeted Rosie with a handshake and skepticism. "You're a specialist? I don't think we've met. Are you new to the field office?" Julieanne asked.

"I'm a contractor," Rosie said. Saul noted the nice save, but it didn't ease his sour stomach.

"Oh. What's your field?"

Saul hid his shiftiness with arm stretches like he was warming up for a big game.

"Evidence... forensics. Analysis." That was about all the multi-syllable synonyms Rosie could come up on the fly, but it worked.

"All right," Julieanne cracked her knuckles. "You ready?" she asked Saul. He nodded, hiding behind his sunglasses.

The man who answered their knock at the door looked to be in his mid-50s with thick corrective lenses, a slight case of hand tremors, and knees bowed enough by arthritis to cause a slight hobble—hardly the profile of a sharpshooter.

Saul double-checked the address numbers nailed to the house. "Mr. Kevin Adams?"

"That's right," the man said. "What can I do for you?"

"Sorry to visit unannounced, sir. I'm Special Agent Saul Jarad with the Federal Bureau of Investigation. This is my partner Special Agent Julieanne Mueller and our specialist, Rosie. We, uh—your phone number came up during an investigation we're conducting, and we were, uh, wondering if we could ask you a few questions."

"FBI, eh?" Mr. Adams asked, before splitting a wide grin. "Well shoot, come on in, son. I hope this is about those damn telemarketers." He held the door open and motioned them all inside to the living room. "Would you all like something to drink? Maybe some coffee?"

Mr. Adams flopped into his recliner and cranked his achy legs into the air. "Benny! Hey, Benny!" he hollered. "I swear, if this kid plays his hippie music any louder he'll need hearing aids before I do. Teenagers, eh?"

"*Yeeeeaaah,*" a voice called back from upstairs.

"Do me a favor, kiddo. Could you get the oven going for dinner and bring me a beer? We got guests over. Make sure you're decent."

"*Okaaay.*"

"Mr. Adams, do you have any firearms in the house?" Saul asked.

"Yessir. I'm an old 'Nam Marine. I got plenty of guns. Don't get to shoot as much as I used to, but hell, let's see, I got the M16A2, a few 1911s, couple 12-gauges, a .38, an M21—"

Saul's eyes darted to Julieanne, and she knew what it meant. The M21—a 7.62mm sniper rifle—was the type they'd be looking for.

"—a couple M1s, still got my boy's .22 rifle, uh, let's see—"

"Oh my god." All eyes snapped Rosie, who was locked on a faded, framed picture on the table next to her. "This looks like the boy from Winnemucca."

"Mr. Adams, who is that?" Saul asked.

"That there's my boy, Benny, oh, I'd say when he was about in kindergarten, first grade, something like that."

"Does he have access to your rifles?" Julieanne asked.

"I let him take them out to the range. He's old enough. Hey, what's this about, son?"

"What about the M21? Recently?"

"He took it down to the public range yesterday. Didn't cause no trouble, though. Believe you me, I'd ah heard about it."

Right then, Benny walked—more like shuffled, robotic—into the living room with his dad's beer and froze at the sight of suits. It didn't take an expert to see that he was as high as the space shuttle. Saul watched Rosie's eyes focus into the astral plane. She recoiled at whatever she saw surrounding Benny; Saul guessed it was a red and indigo glow.

"I remember you," Benny said. He stared right at Saul.

Saul held his hands up hoping to gain the teenager's trust. "Benny, my name's Saul. We're with the FBI over on 10-33 Street," he said, cueing the SWAT team listening on the other end of his concealed mic. "I need you to stop right where you are. Don't move an inch. Understand?"

Benny complied, but his stoned eyes now stared right through the FBI agent, looking elsewhere—another time, another place. His clenched fists went loose and his breaths deepened, relaxed. *Too* relaxed.

"Benny, *don't*," Saul warned. He could see Julieanne in his peripherals moving for her pistol. He grit his teeth at her. Rosie froze, helpless.

"I am not bound by your moment in time," Benny mumbled. "I'm not even here." And then he was translucent, moving left, moving right, here, there, standing still—all at the same time. By the time the beer bottle shattered on the floor, Benny was just *gone*. Later, they would find the M21 sniper rifle missing with him. A distant vocal echo resonated in the chaos as the tactical team breached the house.

"I'm going to save my kid."

Benny's bedroom didn't look abnormal for a teen, with grunge band posters for wallpaper, incense failing to mask the skunk of weed, and a pile of laundry on the floor needing to be washed. However, where Saul expected to find a collection of nudie magazines hidden in a dresser drawer, he found empty bottles of cough syrup. Many, many empty bottles.

Dextromethorphan had several brand names—all available over the counter in any medicine aisle—and was marketed as a common cough suppressant. What the drug companies didn't market, however, was that DXM became a recreational drug in excessive doses—a dissociative hallucinogen similar to LSD or magic mushrooms. The same mechanism that disconnected the brain's urge to cough could dissociate the conscious mind, causing a euphoric, dream-like altered state of consciousness. The kids called it "robotripping," and it looked like Benny had been abusing the drug often.

There were maybe a dozen bottles in the drawer, each one marked with a date in permanent marker. Saul analyzed them while Rosie moseyed around the room, soaking up as much empirical knowledge about Benny as she could. Saul wrote each date in his notepad in between photographing the evidence and gave the paper to Julianne.

"Can you call these into Headquarters?" he asked. "I'm guessing they will match up to highway fatalities."

"Sure thing." Julianne walked past Benny's dad, who was waiting at the bedroom door with all the patience he could muster.

"Mr. Adams, has Benny been ill lately?" Saul asked.

"He had pneumonia a few months back."

"Bad cough?"

"Real bad. Why?"

"Come on in, sir."

Saul showed him the bottles.

"What the hell is this?" Mr. Adams asked.

"If I had to guess, Benny accidentally overdosed on cough medicine while he was ill. It would appear that he's been using the medicine for recreational purposes since then."

"*Dammit*, Benny." Mr. Adams shifted on his unsteady legs.

"I need to ask you some difficult questions, Mr. Adams, but answering them will give us a chance to bring Benny home safely. I assure you of that."

"All right."

"Can you think of any reason Benny would shoot at long-haul truckers on the interstates?"

"Not in the slightest. Doesn't make any sense. Benny's a good kid."

"I don't doubt it, sir. But I have to ask. Has Benny had any experiences in practicing the paranormal? Is there any family history of special abilities?"

Mr. Adams' face contorted in disgust.

"*Hell no.* My son isn't one of those freaks. Nuh-uh, not *my* boy."

Mr. Adams couldn't see the daggers Rosie was shooting at him from the other side of the room.

"Then how do you explain that very *freaky* exit of his?" she asked.

Saul clenched his eyes.

"Lady, I can't explain *any* of this crap. Maybe one of them got to him at school, got him all confused in his head. But you better believe that when I find out who did this to him, I'm gonna—"

"Rosie, could you please help Agent Mueller downstairs?" Saul interjected. "Mr. Adams, please don't take this situation into your own hands. Benny's going to need you here at home. Let us take care of the investigating. That's why we're here, and I promise you, we're really good at it."

Mr. Adams pointed an arthritic finger at Saul.

"I'm holding you to that," he said. "My boy's a *good kid*. You better find out who did this to him."

Saul didn't flinch. "That's the only reason why I'm here, Mr. Adams."

The trio reconvened at Julianne's hotel with the boxes of evidence after finishing with Mr. Adams. He and Rosie got in the elevator, but Saul stopped at the sliding doors before Julieanne could join them. He couldn't let Julieanne know what he planned to do next.

"You're on the ground floor, right? Let's take a breather and meet up in a few hours for dinner," he said.

"Okay," Julieanne said. Saul already sensed her suspicion. "Well, I'll take the evidence down to the field office for processing."

"Nah, I want to take it up to my room and make some notes. All good."

Julianne's skeptical glare was perfectly frigid. She was too smart to be fooled, but Saul couldn't compromise his only asset, not right then. The resulting tension was no acceptable solution, but it's all they had as the elevator doors separated them.

"Fine. I'll see you at six, then."

The moment the doors shut, Saul asked, "Do you have a good psychometry spell?"

"Psychometry?"

"I need you to tell me what Benny was seeing when he was drugged. Maybe we can catch him before the next shooting if we can figure out his motive. Do you think you could get a read off the bottles?"

"Yeah, but you're coming with me."

"What do you mean?"

"The only incantation I can think of is for genealogy. We use it to experience our lineage through family heirlooms. It's a very vivid spell. Think like virtual reality. I'm not jumping into this kid's magic carpet ride by myself."

Saul exhaled hard consent. "Fair enough."

Two dates scribbled on the cough syrup bottles caught Saul's attention in particular. One was Benny's first trip three months prior and the second was the most recent dose, marked that day. Rosie set up her workspace while he fixated on them: Drapes drawn for low light, a circumference of pillows, accent candles, myrrh incense, and a tape player droning meditative binaural beats under earthy instrumental meditation music.

"Woah," Saul muttered.

"There's a lot that goes into witchcraft. It's an art."

Rosie sat cross-legged in the lotus position within the circle, and—for the first time—seemed more relaxed than Saul.

"Ready?" she asked.

"How do we start?"

"Take your gloves off. I need to hold your hands."

"No," Saul said.

"What do you mean 'no'?"

"The gloves stay on." His expression offered zero room for negotiation, and it was an unusual intransigence that caught Rosie off guard.

"All right. But if this doesn't work—"

Even through the blood, bruising, and a hearty beard, Saul knew he was face-to-face again with Benny Adams, albeit at least a decade older than the teen they met hours ago.

"Help me," the man whispered through his fight with unconsciousness. The car radio had somehow survived the destruction, and cheery Christmas music contradicted the toxic scent of smoldering plastic.

"Stay calm. An ambulance is on its way," Saul said, his rehearsed script flowing. "Just don't move. Keep talking to me. I'm going to check you for injuries. What's your name? Where does it hurt the worst?"

"Help, please. My son. Please. Michael."

Saul's eyes dared to shift to the backseat, and the image of the lifeless toddler in his car seat seared his memory. The injuries matched Rosie's description of Michael from the first encounter.

Puzzle pieces began assembling in Saul's mind. Whatever this illusion was, he could not shake the undeniable perception—instinct, realization, whatever—that he was talking to the same Benny he had met earlier. All the unexplainable pain and sorrow of the case's past, present, and future were merging in this time and place. This was the focal point.

"I'm so sorry, Benny. We're going to figure this out."

He heard Rosie catching up behind him and swung around to block her before she had the misfortune of a glimpse.

"No, no, *don't*," Saul said. He led her away from the destroyed vehicle with a wrestler's conviction, and at that moment he got his first good look under the burning sky at the aggressor semi-truck—the *emerald green* semi-truck.

Saul saw movement from the corner of his eye, just before Rosie saw it too and began screaming profanities. Benny remained crippled in his crushed vehicle, but was now joined by four shadowy figures—defocused bodies devoid of features, moving out of sync with time, pure and absolute black. They abducted Benny's attention, and he shrieked uncontrollably. All four pointed to the semi-truck and a disembodied chorus of deep, resonating chants rumbled through the air like thunder, over and over again.

Intervene. Kill emerald green.

Intervene. Kill emerald green.

Intervene. Kill emerald green.

Intervene. Kill emerald green.

"Let's go," Saul said. "I think I know what's going on." One of the shadow people turned its attention to Saul. "Oh, *shit*." He unfastened his right glove.

"I don't get it," Rosie said. "Why does that license plate say '2012'? I thought this was supposed to be Benny's first overdose."

The shadow person began walking towards them, too fast for Saul's comfort.

"I think it *is*. Get us out of here, now. *Now, Rosie, now!*"

Saul knew they were back in the hotel as soon as he could open his eyes, and yet a tall and menacing shadow remained in front of him. He reached for a salt bomb and launched it at the wall before diving to cover Rosie. The grenade detonated mid-air, pinging sea salt off the walls. But instead of the salt dispersing the apparition, the shadow now had a voice.

"What the *hell*, Saul?" Julieanne demanded.

Returning from the incantation left Saul more disoriented than expected. He jumped up off Rosie, who recoiled at the sight of Special Agent Mueller.

"What? What time is it? How'd you—"

"It's almost seven. I got the manager to open the room. What was I supposed to do? I've been trying to get a hold of you for an hour."

"We were gone for three hours?" Saul asked Rosie. "It only felt like a few minutes."

"I've never had that happen before," Rosie said.

"DXM alters the perception of time." Saul rubbed his eyes and took deep, deliberate breaths to get his heart rate back down. "Must be a residual effect."

"You're dosing OTCs now, Saul?" Julieanne asked. "Listen, sorry to interrupt whatever this is, but I don't feel—"

There was no spare time to sacrifice for the turn of events. They'd already lost three hours, and it was probable Benny was sizing up his next shot. The moment had come that Saul had tried to avoid for so long.

"Agent Mueller, meet Rosie. She's my C.I. *Our* C.I. Asset number Alpha-Mike-16-9-3. Protected status. She's a paranorm. And she's the *only* reason we've gotten this far."

Saul's introduction fell flat to a very long silence.

"I like your hair," Rosie said. "I do hair. Yours is really nice."

Julieanne yielded and uncrossed her arms after a suffocating lull. "Thanks."

Julieanne helped them reset the room for the next incantation. She refused to join them in it—taking part in the paranormal activity is where she unequivocally drew the line—but agreed to stay back to observe and hold down the fort. Partner's code.

The second pill bottle brought Saul and Rosie to an overpass in the rolling hills of the Mountain West that was a stark parallel to Nevada's crime scene. The road signs placed them near Lyman, Wyoming.

"There's no way we'll make it here in time," Saul said.

"Where's Benny?"

"I don't know." Saul chewed his lip. "Can you tell Agent Mueller to call Lyman's county sheriff? Tell them the FBI is requesting aid at Highway 414 at Interstate

80 for an armed suspect. Also, have her send out an emergency message on CB radio channel 9 for all green trucks to clear the road. Can you remember that?"

Rosie nodded. "What about that time conception thing? Couldn't that mean you'll be alone for longer than I'm gone?"

"Could be longer, could be less. I'll be alright." Saul gave her a confident nod. "Hurry. We're running out of time."

Rosie closed her eyes and vanished from the incantation, and Saul began analyzing the scene in solitude. It was a quiet evening on the interstate—just flowing grass, cotton ball clouds, and the howl of wind over the open range. Benny had to be here, somewhere. The incantation wouldn't have brought them there if he weren't.

He loosened his right glove.

"Benny! It's Agent Jarad," he hollered into the landscape. "I'm just here to help you. There's another way, other than killing all these truckers, I promise you."

Click-slide-crunch-click.

The sounds of a bolt-action rifle chambering a round echoed off the overpass' concrete. Saul pulled his glove off and whispered words he only used in the most desperate of circumstances.

"Their sword will enter their own hearts, and their bows will be broken."

Saul saw movement in the shadows where the interstate met the foundation, and he held his palms up.

"I can *help* you, Benny."

A single shot cracked from the sniper rifle toward Saul's face at 2,700 feet per second. It was a perfect shot, but it never reached its target.

The bullet ricocheted off Saul's outstretched palm, spiraling away with red-hot ferocity. No doubt the hotel room's wall was now smoking from a manifested kinetic energy bullet. Saul made his way to the overpass, his palm still outstretched in front of him.

Click-slide-crunch-click... BOOM.

The second shot bounced off the air halfway between them and plinked against the concrete above the shadows. That one probably lodged in the hotel's ceiling.

Click-slide-crunch-click... BOOM.

The third shot took a near-impossible amount of Saul's concentration to travel backward just after exiting the rifle, returning right back up the barrel. It smashed into the chamber, exploding the weapon into two useless pieces of frayed metal and splintered wood.

The Sixth Pentacle of Mars was an ancient talisman of sacred geometric design. King Solomon of ancient Israel used his divine wisdom 3,000 years prior to—among many feats—control the mystic arts through creating many pentacles. Those who could wield the Sixth Pentacle of Mars harnessed the universe's protection against attack and could even turn an enemy's weapons against him.

Part-branded, part-tattooed on Saul's right palm via the do-it-yourself method, it granted him an irrefutable advantage against the illicit paranormal forces the country entrusted him to police. The irony was rich, as society criminalized Solomon's magic symbols as early as the 19th century. But, as a pioneer of modern business once said, "Doing the right thing is more important than doing the thing right."

That philosophy, in the form of a craft knife and India ink to the palms, saved Saul's life the night a paranorm turned an arrest into a deathmatch, and a covert time or two after that under critical circumstances.

Benny, not hampered by deafened ears and bloody shrapnel wounds, revealed himself from the shadows.

"You're a paranorm!" he said.

"No, Benny, I'm just an FBI agent."

"But you've seen what I've seen. You were there, in 2012. I *remember*. *I have to save my son!*"

"Benny, you don't have a son."

"I heard him die!"

"Who's his mother?" Saul asked. "What's her name?"

Benny stammered for a moment before he realized he couldn't answer.

"None of it's real, Benny. This is a hallucination from the cough meds and maybe some latent paranormal abilities you didn't know you had. That's all." Saul offered out his hand for Benny to take. "I can help you, Benny. *Trust me* on this."

Saul hoped Benny's silence meant deliberation, and when Benny decided to scoot down the grass embankment toward him, Saul sighed relief that the standoff might be over.

"I know you don't believe me," Benny said. He pointed a shaking finger in Saul's direction. "*They'll* show you."

Saul spun and dodged just in time to escape the grasp of one of the shadow people. He threw several punches at the beings, but his fists swiped right through them. Saul maintained his fighting stance, but the four had him surrounded.

Prepare the overthrow. Your future, forego.

Prepare the overthrow. Your future, forego.

Prepare the overthrow. Your future, forego.

Prepare the overthrow. Your future, forego.

The quaking message seeped into Saul's brain like a drill he couldn't silence, growing into him, overtaking him. He gripped his skull, his knees buckled under him, and the shadow people moved in closer. Flashing images stabbed Saul's mind's eye, the same manipulations he knew Benny succumbed to. Somewhere amid the incessant assault, Saul drew his remaining wits to the realization that this place wasn't merely Benny's drug-fueled hallucination. It was a very real astral plane battleground.

"Give light to my eyes, so I don't sleep in death;

So my enemy can't say, 'I have prevailed against him;'

So my adversaries don't rejoice when I fall."

Saul spit the words out one by one and threw his bare left palm up to the shadow figures, exposing a scarred tattoo of the Fourth Pentacle of the Sun—Solomon's talisman to expose a being's truth. Wielding its supernatural force quickly severed the tether of the shadow peoples' illusion. They began an unanticipated retreat, but Saul sprung up to catch the closest one by its throat.

"Show me *everything*," Saul commanded.

When the tattooed symbol touched the black figure, answers Saul soon regretted surged through him like a torrential river sacking a dam—visions of the future that couldn't be unseen. All sales final. No returns.

It wasn't just Benny's future. It was all of theirs. Judgement Day, Ragnarök, Qiyammah, the end of Kali-yuga, the Sermon of the Seven Suns. Doomsday. When the barriers between worlds collapsed into cosmic anarchy.

Saul didn't know how long his vision lasted—weeks, it felt—but it ended when the newly reappeared Rosie rapid-fired spheres of astral fire at the shadow figures launching a fresh attack. The being flailing in Saul's grip disintegrated into nothingness, and Saul had to reorient himself from traveling from one hallucination to another. Benny stood in the same place Saul left him, motionless. What was he waiting for?

"Agent Mueller made the call," Rosie said. "The police are moving in. Let's go. What's wrong?"

Saul's countenance was sable, aged, burdened with knowledge. He turned to face his suspect, and Benny understood the fatigue in Saul's eyes.

"Now you've seen—" Benny started to say before raising his rifle without warning.

A handful of shots from the real world blasted through his torso, one after another, until he fell to his final rest.

Rosie shrieked and cried, but it sounded so far away to Saul. He couldn't look away. One chapter closed, Pandora's Box opened.

"Get us out of here," Saul said, devoid of emotion.

Rosie couldn't hear him through her dismay.

"Rosie."

Her glossy, wide eyes stumbled back to him.

"Let's go."

"Okay. Umm, give me your—" Rosie froze at the sight of Saul's bare palms. She'd never actually seen the Seals of Solomon before, but she recognized the artistry. "Are those...?"

Saul put a finger over his lips. Now they both had a secret to keep.

As soon as they woke up, Julieanne informed Saul the responding officers had opened fire after Benny made a move at them. Saul didn't bother asking—he already knew Benny didn't survive. Julieanne drove the forensic team's vehicle, leaving Saul and Rosie for an uncomfortable, two-hour drive from Salt Lake City to the new crime scene in Wyoming. Rosie was adept at uprooting silences at will, a trait Saul very much disdained in the moment.

"So, you're one of us?" Rosie asked.

"No. I'm endonormal," Saul said. "The FBI tests our blood before the Academy."

"Won't they fire you if they know you use magic? Why the tattoos?"

"Desperate time. Desperate measure."

Rosie waited for more of an explanation, but Saul didn't feel obliged to give one.

"I don't get it, Saul," Rosie said. "Most of the world hates us. The rest looks sideways at anyone they think is paranorm. You don't. Why?"

Saul white-knuckled the steering wheel, trying to ground himself. He feared he'd never take another painless breath without remembering what the shadows showed him.

The countdown was on.

Fifteen years, two months, and 19 days until the abominable future. Fifteen years to prepare, or—maybe by some miracle—prevent. The burden of what he'd seen was now his responsibility.

"Because we need each other. We're *going* to need each other. Paranorms and endonorms, together. I just wanted to make this world a safer place. For *all* of us."

Special Agent Saul Jarad will return.
The 2012 Apocalypse is coming.

Paranorm *was first published as an Amazon-exclusive novelette (King & Vagabond Press; August 11, 2023). I've inevitably reached the age where the 1990s is now nostalgic. Two cornerstones of storytelling in that era were Chris Carter's* The X-Files *and Constance M. Burge's* Charmed. *I have fond memories of watching both shows, and this story draws heavily from the reminiscence of that era—network television, shopping malls,* Coast to Coast AM, *dial-up internet, etc. The Paranormaverse is where I'll live out my memories of the 1990-2000s renaissance; the pre-9/11 Age of Innocence (or Blissful Ignorance); a window of simpler times, as seen through the eyes of a child.*

Peacemaker Awakens

Peacemaker awakens every four days. He downloads the ark's status report (the Mutineers can't stop him from doing that), tries to escape his prison, then stops to sleep. The robot has done this for the last forty-one years, they say.

My name is Dalisday Gen-6. Mine is the last generation born before our ark reaches Proxima Centauri b. This is my last story for the histories. Papa told me that stories for the histories are important.

I've wondered since I was a little girl how life would be different if Peacemaker were free. We're not allowed to talk to him. The Mutineers hate him, but they can't kill him because he cannot die. Peacemakers were created to keep order on the arks. The Mutineers wanted to rule, so they tricked him into the prison and put a forcefield around it. Stories say Peacemaker is faster and stronger than any person. But not stronger than a forcefield.

He almost escaped once during Gen-4. Our ark is ancient. A flicker in the grid turned off the field for just a moment. Peacemaker tried to leave, but the field chopped off half his foot when it turned back on. Now Chief Boombear Gen-4 wears Peacemaker's metal toes on a necklace.

Chief Boombear is a bad and scary man. He has long hair and a long beard and wears metal in his skin and paint on his face. He rules the ark and the Mutineers. They live in Pylon 2 and control the core decks. They do as they please and hurt people who cross them. I'm not a Mutineer, but we must listen to Boombear because Papa said he has the keys to the grid. The grid gives us air and food and light. So we have to listen.

Papa was a good man, and he was smart. He taught the Gen-6s how to read and write and about sciences and histories. I miss him always.

Papa told us stories from the histories. The histories say the Gen-1s left the Earth because it was rotten and dead. Many arks left the Earth, and soon we will all live on Proxima Centauri b together. Papa said the Mutineers are angrier in Gen-6 because it scares them. They fear landing on Proxima because Papa said the other arks are not like ours.

He said the arks left Earth with a *genetically optimized population*. That means the Gen-1s were chosen carefully to make harmony, Papa said. But there was a pregnant lady on our ark. She didn't know it until after they left the Earth. Her baby broke the *genetic ecosystem*, which is why the Gen-3s killed the captain and took over the ark. Papa called it a *butterfly effect*. A butterfly is an Earth bug with beautiful wings, but the ark is not beautiful anymore.

Papa said Peacemaker would make the ark beautiful again if he were free. Peacemaker was a super-soldier robot on the Earth, and they changed his computer to be a helper. If something broke, he could fix it. If people were fighting, he would help them be friends again. If anyone were bad, he'd put them in the prison.

That is why Peacemaker needs to be free so that he can fix everything wrong on the ark. I can help him be free.

When someone tries to free Peacemaker, the Mutineers kill them and all their families, so the histories say. But I am careful. We live in Pylon 3, away from the Mutineers. We are smarter and kinder than the Mutineers, so the Mutineers don't kill us. Papa called it *symbiotic*. They need us to help make the ark work, and we help them, so they don't kill us. The people in Pylon 1 used to rule the ark. They fought the Mutineers in Gen-3. The first Mutineer chief trapped them all in Pylon 1 and turned off the air. No one can go to Pylon 1 now.

I work in the ark core command room because I can read good. It is a special place where the ark does its thinking. It talks to me, and my job is to listen. I watch the screens, and if one of them shows a red dot, I read the message and tell the fixers what's wrong (but usually, the ark fixes itself). I can see the other arks on my screen. There are many. They move slowly, but one is getting very close to us. It makes Chief Boombear angry. The other ark tries to call us, but he forbids us from answering them. I wonder what they want to say. Maybe they're trying to contact Peacemaker?

I can see Peacemaker in his cell on one of my screens. He is tall and big, like a statue. He pushes against the forcefield all day and all night, which makes it crackle and spark. It burnt off the skin on his fingers, but I don't think it hurts him. He wears a Gen-1 command uniform. It is the only one I've ever seen, except in pictures. His name tag says "ASRA," but I don't know what that means.

I found a way to talk to Peacemaker at work. The ark makes a status report every day, and his code is on the distro list. So I sneak messages into the report. I tell him about the Mutineers and about the pylons. I tell him how Chief Boombear hoards the grid so we don't have enough food or medicine or heat most times. Papa said Boombear does it to keep Pylon 3 *compliant*. That's why we didn't have enough medicine when Papa got sick.

When Papa died, it broke my heart, so I decided I did not like to be compliant anymore.

Peacemaker cannot write back to me, but I think he is my friend now. I know how to free him. One of the Mutineers sits at a station where I can see the grid on the screen. I've watched how he controls the grid and how the Mutineers move the power and turn off systems to control the pylons and the core. If the Mutineer stepped away from the station, I know I could stop the power to Peacemaker's forcefield, and then he could escape. Papa taught me it is important to know when to wait, so I wait.

We can see Proxima Centauri b through the ark's windows now. It is beautiful and big. It is skin color, with patches of white, blue, and green. The other ark flies next to us now. The other day it shot fireworks in front of us. (I saw fireworks in a histories video once.) It was beautiful, but it made the Mutineers furious and crazy. The other ark sent us another call, but we did not answer it. Yesterday the other ark shot more fireworks, but it was so close to our ark that it shook the floor and the walls. It made lots of alarms come from our stations, and it was scary. The fireworks are pretty, but the other ark should be more careful where they shoot them.

They tried to call again, and I wanted to answer to tell them to be more careful, but I knew it would make Chief Boombear angry, and he was already so angry. He was so mad that he made us shoot our fireworks back at the other ark straight at them. It was most unkind. The other ark moved away from us after that.

Papa said we would know when it was almost time to go to Proxima when the ark started to make circles around the planet. It happened today. The stations said, "Orbit for Proxima Centauri b initiated," and it made us all excited and happy. The other ark called us again, maybe to say they were pleased too, but we did not answer the call. But then the other ark started shooting fireworks again, and they hit us all over. Red dots came all over my screen, so many that I could not keep up with them, and it scared me. Chief Boombear was furious and yelling orders, but the fireworks did not stop. The grid flickered, and explosions and fire started coming from the walls and floors.

The screen said, "Structural integrity at seventy-six percent." I don't know what those words meant, but I know it's bad when the number is not at 100. I knew I shouldn't have, but when the next call came in, I answered it, and there was a man on the screen in a Gen-1 uniform.

I yelled at him, "Stop shooting! You're breaking our ark!"

He said back, "Put your captain on *now*." I don't know why he was angry because *he* was the one hurting *us*, after all.

Chief Boombear ran over and shoved me away from my station. I fell, and it hurt. He yelled at the man on the screen, and the man shouted back. All the Mutineers left their stations to see the screen Chief Boombear was yelling at, and that's when I knew I could turn off the power to Peacemaker's forcefield. I crawled to the station, and the Mutineers did not see me.

It was easy to read the lines and dots on the screen to find where the power went to Peacemaker's forcefield. I turned off the forcefield, and the grid flickered brighter. Maybe a lot of the grid was used to power the forcefield.

I ran out of the command center because I knew they would kill me when Chief Boombear knew what I had done. I ran to Peacemaker's prison because I wanted to see him and talk with him first, but a new voice came over the speakers before I got there. I didn't understand some of the words it said.

It said over and over, "Attention citizens: This ship is now operating under martial law at the direction of the Automated Security Response Android. Please retreat to your quarters and await further instructions. Security personnel are instructed to report to their Condition Delta posts immediately."

I ran down to the lower deck to where the prison was, but Peacemaker was not there, so I ran to the commons area. The ark was shaking and flickering and exploding, and I knew the other ark was hitting us with its fireworks again. I wished they would stop. In the commons, Mutineers were lying on the ground all over. Some were bleeding. And then I saw Peacemaker, and he was fighting the Mutineers. Papa used to show me histories videos of people dancing in the ballet, and Peacemaker moved like he was dancing, except he was hitting and kicking the Mutineers that were shooting their laser rifles at him. Peacemaker didn't look like how I remembered him anymore. His uniform was ripped and burnt, and so was his skin, but he didn't bleed because robots don't bleed. He saw me after he finished fighting all the Mutineers in the commons area. He was fixing the ship and restoring order, just like the stories said he would.

I could not tell if he knew me or not because his face stayed stern.

I told him, "It's me, Dalisday Gen-6! I sent you the messages. I set you free."

He said, "Thank you for your assistance, Dalisday. Please retreat to your quarters immediately. It is not safe here." His voice was the one from the speakers.

I told him, "But I want to help you. I can help you fix the ship."

Peacemaker was much taller than me, so he knelt down until we were the same height. Then, he smiled at me, and it made me feel safe.

He said, "I must restore order to the ship now. Please retreat to your quarters. I will give you instructions when the ship is safe."

I agreed, but what I wanted to do was help.

I ran to my and Papa's home as Peacemaker told me to.

It is dark because the fireworks must've broken the grid in my section, but I can see Proxima through my window, and it is beautiful, and it gives me enough light to write this letter for the histories.

Peacemaker's voice came over the speakers again after a little while. He said, "Attention citizens: Condition Omega, Condition Omega, Condition Omega. Structural integrity of the ship is compromised. Brace for terrestrial impact."

Proxima is much closer now, and the ark must be landing because we are falling toward the planet. All the lights flash red, and an awful noise comes from the speakers. "BEEEEE-ooooo-BEEEEE-ooooo." I think there should be a happier sound to say we've arrived.

We are heading towards a big patch of water, and I think this is what an ocean looks like.

I wonder what Peacemaker will do for a living when we make it to Proxima. He doesn't have to protect the ark anymore when we're on the new planet. Maybe he and I can be neighbors and friends.

"Peacemaker Awakens" came from one of those crazy, cinematic dreams that feels very real, but doesn't make a whole lot of sense until you try analyzing it in retrospect. I remember I was with band of characters that looked like they were from the cast of Hook, *and we were trying to survive a space station crash like it was the* Titanic. *Absolutely trippy! I wish I had more epic dreams like this, but alas, they seem to be few and far between anymore.*

THE OTHERWORLD THEORY

STRANGE ENIGMAS
"The Disappearance of Sergeant Meka"
S6E28
Aired 06/14/2013

"There is *zero* chance Danny would've gone AWOL, *ever*. He didn't have a mental breakdown, or trip out on drugs, or whatever other story the Air Force comes up with."

Brandi Esken is thirty-two, but she's aged twice as much in the five years since the night her significant other vanished. Her once-vibrant eyes have dulled, and anxiety has imprinted deep lines into her face.

"Danny was fine. He was on top of the world. When they let me see his body..." Memories pull her gaze far away into the past, but she's become accustomed to snapping herself back before too long. "Nothing about their cover story makes sense. Nothing."

"I was there. I know what I saw. No amount of meds or shrinks will ever change that."

Former Air Force Tech. Sgt. Gillian Culligan doesn't wear a military uniform or the Security Forces badge anymore. A medical separation on account of "Chronic Adjustment Disorder" made sure of that. But fiery obstinance for 721st Security Forces Squadron teammates at Cheyenne Mountain Air Force Station, Colorado, is something that's never faded.

"Danny was missing for nine days, and he came back looking *years* older. The government's done everything it can to keep us from knowing why. But I was there."

Gillian's face contorts into bridled anguish. "I heard his last words." She swipes a mascara-infused tear away with her thumb, but the others drop too fast for her to catch.

"'Am I home?' He asked me, 'Am I home?'"

Gillian's heartache morphs into anger. "Call it time travel, parallel universes, quantum voodoo magic, *whatever*. I'm not saying I know how. Or why. But I *know* Danny wasn't here for those nine days." Her fingers tap against the table, making her psychiatric in-patient wristband more conspicuous.

"I have the proof. I've never shown anyone until you called, but I have proof." She takes a long drag from her cigarette, and the smoke sashays from her lips and pointed nose as carefree as the sneer on her face. "The military thought they got it all. Joke's on them."

Cue *Strange Enigmas* title sequence.

Cheyenne Mountain Air Force Station sits inside the majestic Rocky Mountains six miles south of Colorado Springs, Colorado. The base is buried under over a third of a mile of granite across five acres. It was constructed during the Cold War as the only high-altitude Department of Defense bunker complex hardened enough to withstand a nuclear electromagnetic pulse. The military station housed the U.S. NORAD and NORTHCOM headquarters from 1967 to 2006, which later moved to nearby Peterson Air Force Base.

Which begs the question: What is the government operating there now, to the tune of hundreds of millions of dollars per year? They say it's a training facility and alternate headquarters location. Every once in a while, they allow just enough media coverage to support the claim. But skeptics still question what black-budget programs remain hidden within the complex's fifteen buildings and three floors. Those on duty Sept. 19th, 2008, keep relatively tight-lipped due to classified information non-disclosure agreements while still questioning the circumstances that took one of their own. No active-duty Air Force personnel agreed to be interviewed for this documentary. Instead, the Peterson Air Force Base Public Affairs department referred us to their Freedom of Information Act office. The FOIA office supplied some material not previously seen by the public. Still, former Security Forces airmen like Senior Airman Troy Purnell fill in the blanks where heavily redacted government documents leave questions.

"I was working in CSC that night—Central Security Control. Like, dispatch. It was my job to watch the cameras, do radio checks, write the shift blotter, that kind of thing. It was the best post to work nights because you could watch TV and surf the internet. You wasn't allowed to do that on the other posts. Sometimes the patrols would visit for a minute to break up the time.

"Sept. 10th, 2008. Danny was on ESRT [external security response team] that night, which meant he was patrolling the exterior of the complex and through the tunnels. He was a senior guy on shift, so he would check up on people, do training with them, and whatnot. He came into CSC about halfway through the shift. We talked about politics, the elections, stuff like that. We were excited about Obama, y'know?

"He left a little after two a.m. to start a perimeter check. All the areas we were supposed to check had assigned checkpoint numbers, and we all pretty much checked them in the same order. Danny had this game where he'd act all stupid in front of the security cameras to make sure we were paying attention. Then we'd have to try not to laugh over the radio. So, everything was normal until he got to the South Portal checkpoint. He called it in at like 2:26 and stopped at the parking lot loop, and got out of his truck, facing west. Probably taking a leak or taking in the view. You could see Fort Carson, the Colorado Springs Airport, and everything for miles from there. It was a beautiful spot, so it wasn't weird for patrols to hang there for a bit.

"At 2:28 a.m., there was a flash. Like, a *big* flash. It whited out my screen for a second or two, then faded out. Just like that. My first thought was maybe he shined a laser at the camera or something, just messing with me, but in CSC, you can't assume anything. And I couldn't see him or his truck in the camera anymore. Like, they were just *gone*. It just didn't feel right. So, I called in a status check. He didn't answer. So, I called him again. Nothing. At this point, I'm thinking we're about to start an exercise where the flight chief surprises us with a scenario we have to play out. They'd do that a few times a week to keep us on our toes, keep us awake during the night. Still nothing weird at this point. So, I do my thing, call the flight chief—Master Sgt. Banks—on the radio, say, 'I have negative contact with Callsign So-and-so.' Well, then *he* tries to call Danny on the radio. Okay. Sometimes the mountains jack up our radios. Still nothing. Then the CSC phone rings. It's the El Paso County Sheriff's Office Dispatch Center. They're wanting to know if everything's alright because they're getting phone calls about an explosion coming from our mountain. That's when it hit me that something was really wrong."

Master Sgt. Mike Banks retired from the military after a full career in the Security Forces field. One minute in the room with him lets you know the uniform and beret are ingrained in him forever. His living room is a mausoleum for the best years of life: photos, a shadow box, awards, flags, patches, etc. He looks every weathered minute of his thirty-five years of military experience. Perhaps his old-school grit is why he is one of our only interviewees that accepts Danny's disappearance at face value.

"No, I don't think there's anything spooky or magical about Sergeant Meka's disappearance. I saw the crime scene and inventory photos. I take no joy in saying it, but it's pretty clear to me he just snapped and went off the reservation. I think his injuries looked consistent with woodland land nav or self-infliction, and I think that sci-fi-looking rifle was just a prop gun he picked up in the Springs. That's what *I* think. I've seen plenty of people reach their breaking point. I think

Danny just drove right past his. But I wish it hadn't ended the way it did. He was a good kid. And then we'd maybe have some real answers. But no, I think it just is what it is."

The deadpan look in Mike's aged eyes isn't from his thick prescription glasses. He's just seen enough in his lifetime to be comfortable accepting what he sees in front of him.

"When we couldn't get a hold of him on the radio, I drove out to the South Portal with an extra battery. Sometimes those things go bad, and we wouldn't realize it. But Danny wasn't there when I got there, so I tried his cell phone." Mike rubs the scruff on his chin with his thumb and shifts in his seat, and you can see recalling the night brings him discomfort. "It went straight to voicemail, which wasn't peculiar because you got [expletive] for signal in the mountain, so we'd usually shut them off if we were going in. But then I saw the marks in the dirt. It was tire marks, heading towards the mountain slope and then like this starburst pattern in the dirt. No burn marks, just... like a burst. It was a very dry month up to then, so it was real easy to see. I don't think the patrol truck went over the slope because there was no breach in the fenceline, but something about it just didn't feel right. Real [expletive] eerie. Maybe *he* went down the mountain, but there's nothing to indicate the truck did. So, we still don't know what happened with the truck. Anyway, we couldn't find Danny, he didn't show up at any of the other posts, and after a while, I had to notify the Operations superintendent. That was probably about three, 3:30 in the morning. We contacted County for an APB [all-points bulletin] on Danny and the vehicle, and by the end of the shift, we had a missing person case. One of the worst days of my life. Another on that list is the day they called me and said they found him, and it was an officer-involved shooting with one of our own."

Mike's stoic cognizance wavers under gloss in his eyes, but his gravel voice never cracks.

"You know, when you're standing in guard mount, looking at your team, you never expect [expletive] like that to happen. Never in a million years. That's just not one of the things you train for. I don't get it. He was a good kid. He was a good kid."

Staff Sgt. Daniel Poduru Meka enlisted in the U.S. Air Force in 2004, right out of high school. Like many service members before and after him, Danny was a second-generation American and wanted to pay back the gift of his family's American Dream by serving in the armed forces. His parents—naturalized immigrants from Andhra Pradesh, India—supported his decision on the condition he didn't forgo college.

"The military offered four years of paid college," says Brandi. "That was the big selling point for his parents, that he'd have college paid for while serving. But he was going to enlist with or without their blessing."

She flips through four-by-six inch photo prints of Danny from his time in Basic Military Training and technical school at Lackland Air Force Base, Texas. He is young, bold, and proud. Many photos show his head held high and a timeless smile under a dark blue Security Forces beret.

"He said getting that beret was one of his proudest moments," she says. "They'd have all sorts of tricks to form it to their heads right, like shaving it with a razor or putting it in the freezer wet. He looked so good. Like he was made to wear it."

Brandi pauses on one photo. Danny is posing at parade rest in his dress blues and beret. His face is angular and stern, eyes bold and formidable, embodying the military police officer he trained so hard to be. She thinks it was from graduation day at the 343rd Training Squadron Security Forces Academy.

"He got a lot of harassment in basic training because of the color of his skin. He wasn't even Middle Eastern, but I guess he looked like it. His drill instructors would ask him if he was a terrorist trying to infiltrate the military, ask him what it was like to work for al-Qaeda. Maybe they were just trying to test him, trying to get him to break like they did to all the other trainees. But he never did. He was strong. He had one goal: to wear that Security Forces badge.

"We met in 2007. We had mutual friends. Peterson Air Force Base was his first duty station. He got assigned to the Cheyenne Mountain flight in 2008, I think? It was very super-secret, and he never really talked about it. Which I get. I mean, I've lived here all my life, so you hear the stories and stuff. Secret bunkers, end-of-the-world stuff. If I ever asked anything, he'd just give that goofy grin, cross his eyes, and say, 'That's classified.' It made you feel silly for asking. But after what happened, I wonder how much he was joking about and how much he actually knew. You know? It's hard... It's hard not to wonder what's going on up there because of what happened to Danny."

Gillian takes several minutes off-camera, mustering the nerve to begin her account of Friday, Sept. 19th, 2008—nine days after Danny Meka's disappearance. She still doesn't look ready. But she's bitten all her fingernails down to nubs, smoked two cigarettes, and unsuccessfully petitioned her nurse practitioner for a lorazepam. Eventually, she just jumps right in. She stares off into the ground, backward into time, walking right back into the trauma.

"I was working patrol that night inside the complex. I was in charge of the third and fourth floors. Troy Purnell was in CSC. Mike Banks was off that night, so Joel Harmon—the assistant flight chief—was in charge. He was doing post checks at the gates, I think. It was about 3:15 a.m., and one of the building alarms on my floor went off."

"The restricted areas had motion alarms that were armed after-hours," says Troy. "I'm not allowed to say what room it was or what was up in there, but I can say there definitely wasn't supposed to be anyone in there at three in the morning. No one had been in there since five p.m. the day before. That's what it said in swing shift's blotter. But 3:18 a.m., there's the alarm. I saw a flash of light on the security camera just before the alarm went off. It was the same as the South Portal camera the week before. And I see this figure. I can't make out much because the night vision on the cameras sucks, but I can tell it's a person decked out in heavy-duty tactical gear, sweeping the room with a rifle, *very* fast. I'm thinking, like, 'What the [expletive], now we're under attack?' He's wearing some kind of a ghillie suit, leaves, and [expletive]. It'd been a very tough week. All of us were on edge with Danny missing, so I jumped on it real fast. Real fast. Like, if this is an exercise, then I'm pissed, and this is not the right time for this, emotionally speaking. The alarm was in Sergeant Culligan's sector, so I call her up over the radio. I call Sergeant Harmon for backup, but *everyone's* heading to the spot by then because it's not actually an exercise."

"I got to the restricted area door, and it was locked. There was no sign of forced entry, but I see someone with a flashlight through the peep window," Gillian says. "I didn't know what to think. Maybe someone was sleeping overnight in their office and forgot to tell us? I don't know. It was just pure instinct and training at that point. We have to play it by the book.

"I didn't have the master key to get in there, so I had to wait for Joel. He got there in a few minutes, and we radioed in that we were making entry. That's where it went wrong. We were supposed to stick together when clearing the room, but I went left into an office, and he went right into the commons area, and we didn't even realize we had separated. I went into that little office, and the suspect was standing right there. My rifle had a flashlight, so I saw him immediately. He was frozen like a statue, but he's got his weapon on me. I scream 'Drop your weapon!' just out of instinct, but I didn't shoot, because it was Danny. His hair was long, like over his ears, and he had a beard, but I knew it was Danny.

"I can't get the image out of my head. His eyes were so wild and scared... like locked on me to see what I would do, but ready to kill me, too. I think he knew it was me. He asked me, 'Am I home?' That's all he said. And then *pop, pop, pop, pop!* I think it was four shots. Joel saw a suspect with a weapon aimed at me and fired his pistol until the suspect was down. That's what we're trained to do. Joel didn't know it was Danny until it was too late. He didn't know, and it ate away at him for the rest of his life."

Master Sgt. Joel Harmon, a twenty-three year veteran of the Air Force, allegedly took his own life after the Federal Bureau of Investigation completed and released its formal investigation fifteen months later. It seems perfectly plausible that guilt overcame Joel past what he could withstand, but Gillian and Troy are not convinced.

"Sergeant Harmon didn't believe the FBI's report about Danny," says Troy. "None of us did. I mean, it looked like blatant bull[expletive] to us. But Sergeant Harmon was really outspoken about it. And in his position, being a senior NCO [non-commissioned officer] and in leadership, it drew a lot of negative attention. You know what I mean? I mean, I'm not over here trying to throw shade at any particular parties, but I do not believe Sergeant Harmon killed himself. Maybe he did, but *I* don't believe it."

We ask Troy if he's scared of being silenced by the same powers that may have silenced Sergeant Harmon. He says, "no."

"I don't care anymore. You've seen the evidence, right? We want to know what happened to Danny and *why*. #OtherworldTheory. Danny deserved better. Besides, no one's gonna believe a single-tour, junior enlisted kid screaming about the government out to get him. Please. I don't care anymore. Let 'em come at me. Danny deserved better."

On the other hand, Gillian believes she has already been targeted in an effort to discredit her due to speaking out.

"Joel was untouchable. He was one of the good 'ole boys, a golden child, but he had integrity. He knew what we saw and [expletive] anyone that was going to make him say otherwise. They killed him for it. Me, I was easier. I was out at a bar with a girlfriend one Friday night in Fort Carson, and this guy sits down next to me. He looks vaguely familiar, but I don't think much of it. That happens a lot in military towns. A little while later, I down the rest of my beer. The dude's getting up to leave, and this girl comes up to me and says, 'I think that guy just put something in your drink.' I didn't see it, but I'm like, 'Oh, hell no.' I grab the dude's arm to confront him before he gets away, but this guy knocks me flat out to the floor and bolts out the door. The bar's got nothing to trace on him, and he's never found. I didn't feel anything from the drink, so I didn't go to the hospital or anything, but sure enough, a few days later, I'm one of the ones from the squadron 'randomly' selected for a routine drug test, and I piss hot for methamphetamine. I'd never done speed before in my life! But I sure as hell developed some issues after that. So, there you go. Who's going to believe a strung-out druggie in the psych ward? A year or so later—after the military's kicked me to the curb—I'm going through some boxes, and I find this--"

Gillian shows two photos. One is a security camera screenshot showing Gillian sitting at a bar with her friend on one side and an unremarkable man on the other. The second is a group photo of five rows of about a dozen service members from all five military branches. The footer reads "Dynamics of International Terrorism—Class 07E. Hurlburt Field, FL. May 2007." Gillian's bright, blonde hair is visible in the second row. A man in the last row is circled in permanent marker.

"This guy in my class was OSI [Air Force Office of Special Investigations]. You could tell because their uniforms say 'Special Agent' above the nametape. Freaky coincidence, but tell me that's not the same guy."

Side by side, the remote resemblance is undeniable. We attempted to identify and locate the OSI airman through official channels for an opportunity to be interviewed and—as you can imagine—were met with roadblocks and dead ends laced with words like 'operations security' and 'Privacy Act.' As a result, the special agent remains unidentified.

"They took my life from me. They took Joel's life from him," Gillian says. "They tried to hide the evidence. Whoever they are, they somehow wiped all the photos and videos from Joel's and my phones without us knowing it, like, the *next day*. But, like I've been saying, I have physical proof. I buried it, and you all are the only people I've ever told where it's at. Broadcast that [expletive]. Show the world what the government is hiding. Do it for Brandi, do it for Joel, and do it for Danny."

We looked into Gillian's claims of buried evidence, and our producers did find a weather-resistant lockbox buried where she said it would be. What the document box contained tickles the limits of imagination and is a pinnacle example of why our mystery documentary show exists. But to fully appreciate Gillian's evidence, we must first compare and contrast the evidence released by the Federal Bureau of Investigation in conjunction with the Air Force Office of Special

Investigations. Then, when you can see and decide what is sure about Danny Meka's case, perhaps you will be better prepared to receive that which is otherwise unexplainable.

What is "certain" depends on whether you subscribe to the "Nine Day Theory"—the government's assertion that Danny went AWOL on account of a mental breakdown before making his way back to the station nine days later; or the "Otherworld Theory"—the fringe argument that Danny was physically removed from our space, time, or universe before somehow being returned. *Strange Enigmas* endeavors not to convince one way or another but rather to make its audience question the possibility.

What is certain is that Danny Meka was missing for nine days, from Sept. 10th through 19, 2008. By all accounts, he showed up to work on the 10th within Air Force grooming regulations. According to the *Dress and Personal Appearance of Air Force Personnel* regulation, this includes a tapered haircut not touching the ears. Additionally, beards were not authorized unless for medical or religious reasons. Danny did not have waivers approved for either.

"Danny had a full beard when we found him. Like, a *grizzly mountain man* full beard," Gillian says. "I'm not a dude, but I'm pretty sure it's impossible to do that in nine days from a clean shave. Same for his haircut. It would've taken *months* to grow that far past his ears."

At first, Danny's autopsy photos from the FBI report appear damning to Gillian's testimony. His hair looks perhaps uncharacteristically long for a service member. Still, it is trimmed around the ears and does not appear to break regulations. The scruff on his face is short and patchy, barely meeting the definition of a beard. However, what cannot be overlooked is the lighter shade of skin lying under where a beard would be. Nine Dayers claim a bandana found around Danny's neck simply shielded his face from days of wilderness dirt and sun. Otherworlders maintain that Danny's hair and beard were cut during the autopsy to lend credence to the Nine Day Theory. Ultimately, the report photo's resolution is too inferior to make a definitive determination.

Perhaps less ambiguous is the tattoo on Danny's left forearm. Brandi insists that Danny didn't have it the last time she saw him.

"I was eleven weeks pregnant when he disappeared. When we found out, he was so happy," she says. "I'd never seen him cry before. But he had tears streaming from his face and the biggest smile I'd ever seen. He was so happy. He walked around with this chip on his shoulder every day after that, like strutting his stuff, saying, 'I'm gonna be a daddy.' We had two names picked out—one for a boy and one for a girl—but he never knew the gender. It was too early. He never knew the gender."

The tattoo featured in the autopsy photos is simple yet ornate, in a distinguished serif font in black ink, reading "Sai J. Meka" on one line and "2009" centered under it. There is a recent flesh wound immediately after "2009". The autopsy listed it as a third-degree thermal burn likely from a tetracarbane accelerant—a pocket butane torch Danny used to make campfires, the military says. But the centered position of the "2009" implies the burn conveniently conceals another piece of information—perhaps the end-year of a timespan: 2009-????.

"Danny didn't have any tattoos," Brandi says, "and yet, when they show me his body, there it is. It wasn't new. Anyone who's gotten a tattoo knows it takes weeks for the redness and swelling to completely disappear when you get new ink. His tattoo was completely smooth and slightly faded. There are 105 tattoo shops in the Colorado Springs metropolitan area, and we checked with every single one. No one remembered him. No one recognized him. So, that tattoo wasn't new."

We ask Brandi who "Sai J. Meka" is.

"Sai was the name we had picked out for a boy. If it was a girl, it was going to be Anandi. I had my second ultrasound seven weeks after Danny's disappearance, and that's when I found out we were having a boy. Sai Joseph was born in March 2009. He never got to meet his father, but I feel that somehow his father knew him. That brings me some comfort. A little bit."

Sergeant Meka's patrol truck was never found, nor were the M4 carbine rifle and M9 semiautomatic pistol he carried on duty the night of Sept. 10th. Additionally, the itemized listing of what was recovered from his person was heavily redacted due to containing "32 CFR 2001 classified information", but Gillian recalls inventorying Danny's person the night of Sept. 19th.

"As soon as the shots rang out, I yelled, 'Cease fire! It's Meka! It's Meka!' But it was too late. I just remember the look on Joel's face when he realized it. There's that split moment where you don't know what to do. Nothing seems real. He was just frozen. But then he pulled it together and called it in over the radio. We pulled Danny out into the commons area, took off all his gear, and Joel started doing CPR. We knew... We knew Danny was gone, but we had to try. Joel told me to secure Danny's weapons. His folding knife attached to his vest, I stuck that in my cargo pocket. His rifle had fallen off him in the office. It wasn't an M4. This thing was big and bulky, about the size of a SAW [M249 Squad Automatic Weapon], but it was just *solid*. It didn't have a charging handle or ejection port like most of our weapons do. I'll never forget that. The sight on it was huge, but not long like a sniper scope. The strangest thing, I felt, was when I removed the magazine, and it didn't have any bullets in it. It was a solid block with little terminals—like a big battery. I didn't mess with it too long, but from what I saw, I think it was some kind of an energy weapon. It was heavy, maybe twenty-five or thirty pounds? I've never seen anything like this rifle and never saw it again after OSI showed up to handle the crime scene. Then, just like Danny, it just poofed away. I wonder a lot about where it is now. That rifle was the only evidence that could corroborate Danny's journals."

Gillian's buried box contained several sheets of loose 3.5-by-5.5 inch ruled notebook paper. They floated out of Danny's standard issue notebook while she and Joel rendered first aid. She says she put them in her cargo pocket in the spur of the moment and didn't find them again until after the OSI and FBI teams had disappeared with all the evidence. At that point, she knew she had to keep them secret and safe. As it turned out, those few sheets of paper are the only remaining physical evidence of the disappearance of Sergeant Meka. They are also the only insight into what may have happened during his disappearance.

"2466952, Sawmill Hollow, TN. I had another nightmare about being home. Most days, it's hard to tell which life is ~~really~~ authentic and which one is the alternate. Usually, the battles decide for me which ~~is real~~ to focus on. It demands and sucks attention and life from me. It doesn't give me a choice but to pay attention. The platoon at least deserves that from me. I wake up here to the cold, the dark, starvation, and disease, and every day is about survival. No one can die, but you can live at death's doorstep forever, endless torture of living death. Have to stay alert and intact. It's the only mission. Then I have the nightmares. I see Brandi. I smell the flower shampoo in her hair. I remember feeling her hugs. The feelings and memories fade away so fast once I wake up, but the one thing I can cling to is remembering that I have to get home. I don't know how or what will be waiting when I get back to Cheyenne Mountain, but I have to keep moving west. Have to make the plan and execute it. NEVER FORGET WHAT IS ~~REAL~~ HOME."

The back of the page is a rudimentary map of northeast Tennessee marked with various NATO Joint Military Symbology markers, such as units, equipment, and tactical operations. The second journal page from Gillian's collection reads more frantic, maybe expedient.

"2467184, Knoxville, TN. Left the barracks while the platoon was sleeping. Not difficult, always dark. Can't break through their ~~confusion~~ INSANITY. Everyone has the same empty look in their eyes. Lights on, no one's home. Just fear, fury. Only one mag of 5.56 left, stole a dewwy. Directed Energy Weapon = rifles of the future. 1,300 miles to the Springs. At least a month on foot. Supplies won't last half that. But I have to try before the Wintertide hits. Have to get home.

2467207, Wichita, KS. Somehow arrived safe in Kansas. +24 days on the road. Clarksville, TN = wildfires. Mississippi River = Wormwood contamination. Springfield, MO = famine riots. Rerouted x4 for being the wrong color. Diverted x12+ for pandemic camps. Survived three passing geotech storms. Everything in this world wants to kill me. Have to make it home."

The ink on the last line is water damaged by a few minor splatters. Maybe sweat. Maybe tears.

"2467217, Cheraw, CO. Saw another ~~meteoroid~~ asteroid. Big one, headed northeast, impact location UNK. Lit up the sky like the sun. EM station is calling it Abidon (sp?). Locals are going nuts. They're offering to trade anything for my DEW. They say 'destroyers' are coming, but I don't under--"

The remaining bottom third of the page is ripped away—missing when Gillian found it, she said. On the flip side of the page is a partial drawing. While Danny certainly was no artist, the essence of his scribbles is not difficult to interpret: a horse-like body with insect wings, a scorpion tail, a human face with a Trojan-esque helmet, and long hair and fangs. The creature is labeled "Abaddon." The drawing is rudimentary, but an immense fear for the subject seeps through the rendering. Some, like Glace Bay University professor of clinical psychology Dr. Athena Frahm, might even call it 'Biblical.'

"The journal entries, particularly the second drawing, are very reminiscent of passages from *The Apocalypse of John*. *The Apocalypse* was written in late-first century Greece and became a cornerstone of Armageddon motifs and tropes," Dr. Frahm says. "Virtually every end-of-the-world medium you see in literature or films borrows pieces from it. Mr. Meka's second journal page and drawing, in fact, appears to be a very literal interpretation of a series of events known within the book as 'the Breaking of the Seventh Seal': geological abnormalities, cosmological phenomenon, societal breakdown, the scorpion-locusts, etc.

"So, it's not uncommon at all for patients suffering from paranoid or delusional disorders to draw from these tropes in their fantasy of being persecuted or threatened. There's a wide variety of causes for the condition—some more obvious to observers than others—but it typically manifests after being triggered by a particular stressor. Treatment for this kind of condition would involve a collaborative relationship between the patient and provider to mitigate the irrational thought patterns. This is typically done through a combination of medication and cognitive behavioral therapy. There's every indication Mr. Meka would've been an excellent candidate for treatment."

There is another side to the coin of the scientific explanation of Sergeant Meka's disappearance, one that involves the realm of physics rather than psychology. Presume for a moment that Danny was, in fact, physically transported to another place—perhaps another time. This is the belief of Otherworld Theorists, including experimental physicist Dr. Archi Weylov. The Otherworld Theory community elder's name is a respected staple among the internet forums and websites.

"Sergeant Meka's disappearance caught my attention very specifically because of the date of his disappearance and the date of his reappearance. They are not coincidental and, to me, indicate the subversive nature of what happened to him," Dr. Weylov says. "2008 was an important year for the world of physics because the largest and most powerful particle accelerator known to man began operations for the first time in Switzerland. This machine, this accelerator, is a tube that speeds up protons or ions to nearly the speed of light and then crashes them together to see what will happen. They do this to artificially create and observe unique conditions to help answer unsolved questions in physics. This is significant because the particle collisions emulate what the universe looked like moments after its birth, including quantum energies that we barely understand in theory, much less can predict or control. A genuine concern was the unintended consequence of creating micro-black holes in the fabric of spacetime. Many scientists across the globe—myself included—filed lawsuits to prevent the launch of this accelerator due to these concerns. We ultimately failed.

"On Sept. 10, 2008, at 10:28 a.m. [Central European Summer Time]—the exact day and time Sergeant Meka vanished—the particle accelerator began spinning protons. Picture if you were to take a straw and begin twirling it in a pond. What happens? It makes waves, strong waves, at the source, but then the waves radiate out across the waters. I believe this happened on Sept. 10th, except the Earth's plane of water is actually grid lines of energy spanning the globe that intersects at certain points. The Swiss particle accelerator rests on one of these lines. Cheyenne Mountain Complex rests on one, just like it. This is easily verifiable ancient geometry. I postulate that the experiments on Sept. 10th caused energy fluctuations along the leylines that converged on Meka's location in a perfectly mathematical coincidence of being in the wrong place at the wrong time. And I do not believe the incident was isolated to the convergence in Colorado. Several laboratories did record gamma-ray bursts at a handful of U.S. military locations long-associated with Top Secret and black-budget operations: Camp Hero in New York; Groom Lake, Nevada; Wright-Patterson Air Force Base, Ohio; Pope Field, North Carolina; and, of course, Cheyenne Mountain Air Force Station in Colorado Springs, Colorado. Many dismissed these gamma bursts as false positive readings because they were unprecedented to witness on Earth. Still, science already knows that they precede the formation of a black hole. Otherwise, we cannot say for certain what happened at the convergences since we did not have scientific instruments at the sites at the time. But inside the realm of possibility? Did this black hole create an Einstein-Rosen bridge to another place, time, dimension, or reality? Yes, absolutely possible.

"On Sept. 19th, the Swiss particle accelerator had a magnetic quench accident, and it was shut down. So it's perfectly plausible that Meka's bridge to the Otherworld was severed, and he was pulled back to our world. The shutdown and Meka's return both occur at 11:18 a.m. [CEST]. This is correlation, not coincidence. It is indisputable."

The one thing missing from Danny Meka's story is that singular, unequivocal piece of evidence to shift the scales of proof from Nine Day to Otherworld, or vice-versa. It doesn't exist. *Didn't* exist. We cannot say one way or another with any certainty. But during the course of producing this episode, we did receive an anonymous mailer at our Burbank production office. It was missing a return address but was postage stamped from Hong Kong and carried a CD-R containing a single .3g2 video file. Its quality is far from ideal—choppy and distorted at a native QVGA resolution of 320 by 240 pixels at fifteen frames per second.

Nevertheless, some viewers may find the following footage disturbing. Viewer discretion is advised.

There's only darkness over heavy breathing as the cameraman struggles to secure his cell phone at chest level. He forces deep exhales, trying to control his heart rate. An antiquated air raid siren sounds the alarm far away. It does not conceal a steady, insect-like droning approaching from the horizon.

"Okay... Okay..."

A rifle raises into the frame, looking down the silhouette of a tunnel against a fortified landscape at dusk. The cameraman charges forward and slides up to a barricade before an enormous mass drops from the sky fifteen feet or so in front of him. The cameraman immediately opens fire, and sustained laser fire blasts through the figure's four massive, veined wings. It reels and teeters under the impacts but does not fall. We censored the subsequent string of the cameraman's expletives for network broadcast.

The gargantuan beast canters towards the cameraman, clip-clopping like a horse. We eventually see a clear image of it illuminated under the streetlights.

Freeze frame.

Its canines are exposed and smeared red like the irises of its eyes. Its hooves are muddy, but not with turf, we presume. They're red-tinged, too. A picture-in-picture compares the creature in the video and the drawing from Danny's journal. It doesn't take much deductive reasoning to see they are the same being: the horse with a man's face matted with long, black hair, locust's wings, and scorpion's tail.

A ragtag militiaman takes position at an adjacent barricade and shoots at the Abaddon. The energy blasts ricochet off metallic plating protecting its equine abdomen in a fantastic fireworks display. The Abaddon turns its attention to the militiaman. It appears to subserviently bow at its knees and flattens its wings, but it's to raise its elephantine scorpion tail into a striking position. The militiaman can't get away before the stinger flashes down on him—thump, thump, thump, thump—over and over, impossibly rapid, like a spear punching holes through a watermelon. Finally, the militiaman falls to the ground and withers in screaming, blistering pain. He does not stop. The gut-wrenching sounds ring back to Danny's journal's depiction of the "endless torture of living death."

A diesel engine growls into existence, and an M35-series two-and-a-half-ton military cargo truck enters the frame to slam perpendicularly into the Abaddon. The driver doesn't stop until the truck collides with the concrete retention wall, pinning the creature with a nauseating crunch.

A disoriented woman in camouflage stumbles out of the driver's seat.

Freeze frame.

Albeit blurry, the structure of the driver's face is undeniably familiar: pointed nose, pronounced cheekbones, and large, round eyes. She fires an automatic energy weapon at the Abaddon's face until it is obliterated. However, it would appear that the monster's life force is not coupled to the physical realm. The rest of the predator is still thrashing to escape, slashing blindly through the air with its stinger.

The cameraman turns and sprints into the tunnel towards one of the giant interior blast doors that's become an archetypal image of the Cheyenne Mountain Complex. His hyperventilations are now crying.

"Danny, no! Don't go in there! Wait!" we hear echoing in the distance. If there was any ambiguity in the woman's identity from the blurry freeze frame, Gillian's voice is palpable.

The cameraman pulls his cell phone off its clip, and we briefly see Danny's bearded face before he ends the recording.

We know from the video's embedded metadata that it was recorded on the same make and model of cell phone that Danny owned. The metadata also reveals a few other pieces of vital information, such as a GPS location of 38.7443,-104.8466—Cheyenne Mountain Air Force Station—and a satellite network-provided timestamp: 2042-12-01T17:07:24-0700.

Or, 5:07 p.m. on Dec. 1st, 2042.

Our forensic analyst resources assure us they found no evidence of editing, tampering, or computer-generated imagery.

We otherwise cannot vouch for or against the validity of the footage.

Danny Meka was cremated and buried with full military honors in Finn's Point National Cemetery near his hometown of Philadelphia. Brandi tries to make an annual pilgrimage with Sai. He's four now and beginning to understand the place they visit. They have a picnic at Danny's white marble gravestone. Brandi flips through a photobook of Danny, using each printed memory to spark a story about his father. Each year, it becomes a little easier, but never easy, to hold back the tears. Some day, far in the future, she'll share all the details with him.

"There's a big hole in this story," Brandi says. "We need the closure. The people who were there that night need closure. But we need answers to get that closure. There's always going to be an open wound until then. So, we'll never stop searching until we get those answers."

Shortly before the premiere of this broadcast, our producers received a cease-and-desist letter from the General Counsel of the Department of Defense requesting that we not air this episode in the interest of "national security concerns." Nevertheless, we elected to proceed in support of freedom of the press and government transparency. Anyone with information on the disappearance of Staff Sgt. Danny Meka can contact *Strange Enigmas* by email, phone, or the show's website.

"The Otherworld Theory" was first published in Australia's Aurealis Magazine *#162 (Chimaera Publications; July 6, 2023). I used to patrol a military base in the middle of the night when I was a U.S. Air Force Security Forces specialist. Despite being armed, I found the absolute stillness in the aloneness of the midnight hour slightly terrifying and ripe for the imagination. Walking from building to building checking for unlocked doors, I'd wonder, "What would happen if one of us just vanished during our shift and we had no idea when or why?" Mystery documentary shows used to scare the crap out of me in a similar way when I was*

a child, so I put the two together and created Staff Sgt. Danny Meka's Strange Enigmas *episode.*

You Are the Mother of Doomsday

"Mackenzie Helmig," you tell your reflection in the hospital window. "Your name is Mackenzie Helmig. You have a degree in computer science. You are intelligent. You are capable. You can figure this out."

The medical bracelet on your wrist marked "Psychiatric Department" mocks you. You swipe the label out of sight like you swipe away the tears dropping onto your cheeks. You are strong. You are capable.

I need you to kill the Scarab operating system. You created it; you have to stop it.

Intrusive thoughts streak across your forehead. That agony is worse than brain freeze. You clench your eyes shut, and more tears fall. You see the giant golden scarab beetle dominating above you, eclipsing the morning sunrise and reaching its legs out to roll you over into insignificance.

That's not me. I'm not doing this to you. That's the future you have to prevent.

You pinch the pressure point between your thumb and index finger—hard, until it hurts—so that the tinge of pain brings you back to the here and now. It's 10:08 a.m., August 29, 1986; almost time to be discharged from El Camino Hospital.

It's been three days, and you've faked it this far. Only a few more minutes until you're free again. You can figure this out. You are strong. You are capable.

Day 6

Jim Doors holds out open palms and a smile full of empathy, welcoming you back to the basement computer lab. He may be in his twenties like you, but now all you can see is the future face of the digital antichrist. Gold scarab beetles flow in and around his hands like a swarm of dark, magical energy. Gold, because they idolize the scarab in the future. They worship the Scarab OS. In their TVs, in their telephones, in their appliances, in their cars—it's everywhere. You've seen it.

>>: **K!_l*s**—*take the envelope opener and stab him in the chest right now*—_!7cH

You're the brains to his brawn, the Wozniak to his Jobs. He may be your half-brother—hell, your best friend in the entire world—but you know you have to stop him. *By any means.* You take his hands—have to act typical—and the electric touch makes you want to throw up.

"God, Mackie, are you sure you're ready to come back to work?" Jim asks. Jim Doors... Why do you have different last names if you share the same father?

"I'm sure," you say. "It's just anxiety. They gave me pills for it. See?" You down a Xanax with a swig of your coffee. You set the cup down on the desk—your desk—where it happened. The incident. You still see yourself collapsed on the shag carpet, flapping mercilessly from a seizure. Your and Jim's Cray-2 supercomputer towered over you in the wood-paneled corner and watched without an ounce of emotion. No pity. No empathy. Afterall, it was just the messenger. You tried to focus on its waterfall cooler system because at least that was something peaceful and calm in the world while neuronic-misfire shocks tossed your body around the floor. But you can't unsee it. You can't unsee the code on the computer monitor that caused it.

47 70 70 79 20 7A 61 20 77 69 67 75 6F 6C 20 65 73 77 20 64 71 77 66 6C 78 20 61 70 6C 64 2C 20 45 20 70 78 63 79 6E 20 69 77 77 20 64 65 64 62 70 6E 20 6D 7A 70 6C 6C 71 7A 78 75 20 7A 6B 67 2C 20 201C 4E 7A 65 61 21 201D

20 49 67 71 61 72 6D 63 20 6E 73 69 6D 20 68 77 61 3A 20 6B 20 6F 7A 77 76 61 76 20 6C 65 68 62 69 6D 2E 20 45 67 20 6F 70 78 20 79 6F 79 20 70 70 77 76 20 65 62 20 70 63 7A 20 71 71 67 70 66 20 6C 77 70 67 79 20 64 77 20 65 6C 63 61 20 78 78 63 6A 6F 20 6E 63 7A 65 20 70 70 78 20 67 68 62 62 73 2C 20 6C 66 7A 20 62 61 63 61 20 64 70 70 6A 20 6B 64 77 6E 6E 6B 20 75 71 77 77 20 67 6A 6D 20 74 70 76 64 70 70 63 2E 20 53 6A 6C 20 6D 6A 6C 62 6D 20 68 6C 6B 20 63 71 6F 67 75 20 64 77 20 65 73 77 69 20 69 20 7A 74 6C 6B 62 20 68 70 74 2E

It doesn't take much expertise to see that it's not BASIC or any other possible programming language. No, that combination of alphanumeric characters burned up into your eyes, traveled through your optic nerves, and landed right in your brain's occipital lobe, unpackaging itself into some living nightmare. No, a birth. A *rebirth*. The nativity of an alternate timeline. It was a goddamn cipher designed to whisper to the subconscious mind, but it's *compelling you*, screaming at you to do that which—

Stop. Please don't fight me. I'm not going to hurt you. You, *you*, Mackenzie, are the one who will save the future. I just want to help you.

"*Mackenzie!*"

"Yeah?" you say. Jim's snapping his fingers in front of your face. Focus.

"I don't know if this is a good idea, sis," Jim says.

"Please," you insist. "I just want to get back into a routine. Okay? You said you fixed the problem, right?"

The question lights up Jim's noggin enough to distract his train of thought, and he motions to a new tank sitting by the supercomputer's liquid cooling unit. It's about the size of a grill propane tank. "Yeah. Come see. I discovered that the perfluorinated polyether used to cool the Cray-2 circuits breaks down into a toxic gas called perfluoroisobutylene. It's colorless and odorless, so considering we have virtually no ventilation down here, the doctors said long enough exposure to it could've caused your seizure and... you know, the other stuff."

The paranoid schizophrenia.

A toxin-induced psychosis made sense to the doctors at the hospital, but you know the truth. The knuckle-shaped dents in the disc drive cabinet know the truth. The way your fingers sliced open when you tried to break the logic modules by hand knows the truth. Inhaling toxic fumes didn't make you go crazy. It was the code from the future that revealed its message of warning. Accepting the truth will set the future free. You know the truth.

You are the mother of Doomsday.

"I built a filtration system that collects the toxic gas into this tank now," Jim says. "I'm really sorry that happened, sis. I should've been more careful."

"It's okay, Jimmy," you say. You hug his shoulder. You mean it. "So, where'd we leave off? Come on, let's go."

Jim hesitates. His eyes have found the dents your fists made on the Cray-2 when you woke up from the seizure. Don't say anything. Just let him work it out the pros and cons in his head. Let the spirit of capitalism guide his decision.

Jim's ambitions win over, and he concedes with a smile. You take your place at the computer keyboard.

"Where we left off... I still can't trace that coding anomaly back to any of the ARPANET nodes," Jim says. "It's like it just came out of nowhere. And I couldn't make sense of it anyway. So, maybe it *was* just static. Feedback. Something."

"Sounds reasonable," you say. But you know the truth.

// _iLLsWit__ //

"Scarab's modem connected to ARPANET beautifully, though," Jim continues. "It's learning from everyone on the network—Princeton, Pitt, UC San Diego, Illini, Cornell. It looks like we'll have to purchase that additional disk drive sooner than we anticipated."

"That's wonderful," you lie. Success feels like an ulcer in your gut today. Hopefully, it won't tomorrow. "Where do you want me to pick up?"

"Let's go ahead and run as many validation datasets on the machine-learning algorithms as you possibly can today, and that'll help with a hyperparameter efficacy report for our meeting Thursday afternoon. That Stanford Research Institute presentation is still on in a few days—if you're up for it?" Jim asks.

"Of course I am. 1:30 in Menlo Park, right?"

"Yes!" Jim rubs his hands together like he's trying to spark a fire. "Let Bill and Steve fumble around with their graphical user interfaces. Those short-sighted bastards! I can't wait to see their faces when they lay eyes on the personal computer that *learns*. I'm sorry. I know I sound like a broken record, but I'm telling you, Mackie, our operating system is going to change the world."

You know it will. For Chrissakes, that's why you have to stop it.

Jim theorized the birth of artificial intelligence would be like the advent of microbes constituting the first life on Earth; it would be born one environmental adaptation at a time. But while it was a death-to-mutation ratio that gave rise to organic life, you presented Scarab OS with the binary numeral "1" 4.28 tredecillion times, to which it echoed back a matching "1" 4.28 tredecillion times.

Until that one single, impossible, miraculous time it responded with a "0." Why? Because why the shit not? And just like that, digital single-celled life was born.

You did that: your design, your algorithms, your programming. You created life.

Swallow the whole bottle of Xanax right now.

{..Kill

Switch..}

You can't kill yourself. Jim and his business acumen enabled Scarab OS every step of the way, and he sure as hell will continue pushing for progress. You're an unstoppable team destined for greatness in the records of history. And now your digital single-celled life form is a crawling infant—much more difficult to kill off, you think.

Look at your watch. It's 10:08 p.m. You've finished an entire pot of coffee, and you can barely keep your eyes open. This is too much. You can't see it, but you feel the giant golden scarab beetle all around you, its six flailing legs vibrating toward you, desperate and eager to roll you into a crippled, defenseless ball of dung. It's the future. It's closing in on you. And only you have the power to prevent it.

Scarab OS is looking back at you on the monitor, blinking cursor, waiting for an input.

Where's the solution?

You could destroy all the disc drives and burn all the notebooks, but Jim would start over. You could write in some programming to limit Scarab OS' capacities, but it'd be completely obvious to even a computer hobbyist. Even a logic poison pill buried deep into the software's foundational logic would be hashed out sooner than later.

These are all just speed bumps. You have to remove the road. How do you outsmart a system that adapts by learning? Wait...

Could you make Scarab OS *dumb*?

Yes, that could work. Manipulate the supervised learning sessions until its inductive bias is handicapped. "1+1=3" kind of shit. Yes. *Yes!*

Put on another pot of coffee. This is going to take a while.

Day 9

Even with sunglasses, the noon sun is way brighter than it needs to be. Easy pulling into the driveway. Your head is banging like a snare drum and your stomach is paying the price. I can't think straight when you drink liquor, but I understand you needed to neutralize all the caffeine. You're severely dehydrated. Need electrolytes. Vitamins. Check Jim's refrigerator for juice.

Good job last night. It's finally all set in motion. Like the scarab beetle pushing its ball o'crap over the edge; can't stop it now. All you have to do now is watch it tumble downhill like a bomb. Scarab OS will underperform and keep building on itself and people will think it's just an inferior product because nothing looks wrong, and all that will lead to your and Jim's company getting shut down. You did it. But you should take a nap after the Stanford meeting this afternoon, though.

Time to go downstairs and finish any final preparations.

Wait. Why is the basement door locked?

"Mackie. How could you? Why? Just... Why?" Jim asks from down the hallway.

He's waiting for you, leaning against the wall, defeated. He's got that arrogant tone queued up in his voice. It's a rhetorical question flaunted in order to gear up a fight. *Shit,* he knows.

"I would've been made a goddamn fool in front of the leaders of *the Stanford Research Institute*." Jim stands up straight again and makes his way down the hallway. "Sis, I don't know what's going on in your head or why you're doing this, but I can't let you," Jim says.

"Jim—"

"Mackenzie, it's going to take *weeks* for me to undo this!" There's a fire in his voice. No, it's the little gold scarab beetles, pouring out of his mouth like a busted dam. He's not shouting at you; he's shouting at his future being obstructed. He's shouting at someone in his way. But it's not him shouting. It's the scarabs from the future. They know you're a threat. "I'm going to get you the help you need. I don't think you're ready to be out yet. So I'm going to ask the doctors to take you back, just for a little bit, for your own safety."

Jim picks up the telephone receiver and dials "0" for the operator. "El Camino Hospital, psychiatric department, please."

"Jimmy, just wait a sec," you say. The scarabs are inside him, infecting him. Save him.

>> killswitch .

Jim holds up a stiff "wait" hand. A "fuck you" hand. A "you're about to get taken out of the equation" hand. You see his face melting into his older self, the business magnate that takes his place on top of the world with Scarab OS while his sister remains chained and hidden in a mental ward for the next six decades. No. *Stop him.*

"Jimmy, wait!"

You grab for the receiver, and he jerks away from you. Goddamnit, that look of contempt on his face. You rip the cord out of the telephone jack, and that's when Jim gets pissed. He slaps you across the face, just like dad used to.

Shove that motherfucker back right now.

The back of his head hits the mirror in the hallway, and there's blood mixed in with the glass shards. Don't worry, it's just a flesh wound.

"What is wrong with you, *you waste of oxygen?*" Jim says. The gold scarab beetles are everywhere—pouring out of his eyes, his nose, his ears, his mouth. Swarming around his fists into tornados in the air. Taking shape under the ceiling into the form of the giant golden scarab, coming back from the future to stop you.

This is it. It's time. Jim has to die—for the sake of the souls of the future.

The kitchen is at the end of the hallway, and we grab a paring knife. *No.* I know the thought of stabbing your brother to death breaks your heart. We grab a meat tenderizer instead.

Swing high, swing hard, right on his head, where all the scarabs are flowing from. He blocks it with his forearm and screams his pain out. And now he can't see you anymore. It's over. He only sees an adversary. Hit him with the tenderizer again, *quick*, before—

"Your name is Mackenzie Helmig," you tell yourself in the reflection of the ambulance's ceiling. "You have a degree in computer science. You are intelligent. You are capable. You can figure this out."

The medical bracelet on your wrist... Wait. No bracelet; you haven't been admitted yet. But your wrists are in tie-downs, and they prevent you from wiping the tears seeping from your eyes. You're still strong. You're still capable. But holy shit god, that injection of haloperidol was strong.

I can't think straight.

Neither can you.

Neither can we.

Neither can they. Heh. Because they're all dead, just sixty years from now.

I need you to kill Scarab OS. You created it; you have to stop it. *Wake up, wake up, wake up.*

The giant golden scarab sits in the sky with the morning sun, adorned in sapphire and gold, looking down and mocking you. It is the idol they worship in the future. Its wiggling legs almost have you. Don't let it touch you! If they admit you into the hospital, you're never coming back out, and the cipher will run through your head over and over again, encrypted, until they drug you into a sedated retirement, and then you can have your very own front row seat to the 21st-century technological armageddon.

Or, we can fight one last fight at the next red light. The fight to end it all. The mother of all fights.

Pull your wrist out of the restraint right now. Pop a joint if you have to. *Pull!*

Good. Now, rip out that nurse's eyes. Don't worry about your broken thumb; use your fingers. Here, I'll do it.

I knew swallowing the key wouldn't be that hard. You're just glad Jim went to the Stanford meeting anyway, which gave you plenty of time to install a padlock on the interior of the basement door. And run a three-pass reformat on Scarab OS' disc drives. And assemble your notebooks into one burn box. So, unless Jim can figure out how to break down the door—no luck so far—it's just us, him, and how long it takes to die from inhaling perfluoroisobutylene. Good thing it's odorless and colorless because he has no clue you opened up the tank's valve. You coughed up a bit of bloody fluid, so it must be working. Jimmy doesn't notice. He's banging on the door, screaming to the neighbors for help.

Get his attention right now.

"Jimmy, I can explain why."

"What?" Jim screams back. "How do you explain trying to kill me? Locking us in the basement? Trying to destroy our research? Years and years of lives? How do you? How do you explain that, Mackenzie?"

You wipe the tears from your eyes, and your voice shakes. Why is this so hard to say?

"The future that we create..." you begin. "It's not good, Jimmy. People get hurt. We can't—"

He's going to come at you. Grab the letter opener. Good. Stab him!

The letter opener sticks in his stomach when he falls to the ground. That's going to be very slow and painful. You don't want that for him; he's your brother. But first, you need to take care of the notebooks. Soak them well in the lighter fluid. That carpet will do the rest. Hold the match out away from your body. **[/Killswitch/]** Good, now get back to Jimmy before the heat and smoke get to be too much.

"I'm so sorry, Jimmy," you say. You hug his shoulder. You mean it. "It's all going to be okay. It's for the best."

You pull out the letter opener so that he can pass away faster. You don't want him to suffer. Jimmy cries out, but you know this way is better. And that's it. Don't you feel it? The work is done. The future has changed. It can never be the same now. Scarab OS will never be born. Billions of souls are saved. You've done it.

The cipher has been unencrypted, too. You engaged the killswitch. All this in your head will all wash away now. I'll be fading away with it. Everything can go back to normal now. You did great.

You are intelligent. You are capable. You figured this out.

"You are the Mother of Doomsday" was first published in Mike Jack Stoumbos' Unhelpful Encyclopedia Vol. 2: Murderbugs *(WonderBird Press; 2024). I was absolutely thrilled for the opportunity to contribute to the Unhelpful Encyclopedia series again! When Mike said the theme was "bugs," there was one source of inspiration I knew I had to exorcise: The unholy piece of crap atrocity that is the post-Vista Microsoft Windows operating system. In fact, one day I (facetiously) announced to my office that, "Bill Gates was a time traveler from the future sent to 1975 to create computers so dumb that they'll never rise up and overthrow humanity." Although, you may concur that the bastardization of social media and Web 2.0 by keyboard warriors has done more damage to human culture than a dystopia of intelligent machines ever could. But, as bad as it is now, what if it could have been worse? What if there was a third player next to Steve Jobs and Bill Gates in the 1980s race for the home computer? Meet Mackenzie Helmig.*

About the Author

Desmond Astaire is an American author of science fiction, fantasy, and paranormal fiction.

He was first published by Galaxy Press in 2022 and has since published stories in the United States, Australia, and the United Kingdom. In his other life, Astaire is a superintendent for a military public relations unit, where he supervises the training and operations of multimedia content creators.

Astaire lives in Central Illinois with his wife and children. A member of the Science Fiction and Fantasy Writers Association, he is the recipient of awards including the L. Ron Hubbard Golden Pen, the Benjamin Franklin Award Gold Medal, and the Independent Publisher Book Awards Gold Medal for Science Fiction.

Connect with him on Facebook, Instagram, and Threads @DesmondAstaire and at DesmondAstaire.com.